Advance Praise for
Remember My Beauties

"In vibrant prose, Lynne Hugo tells a gritty, psychologically astute story of three generations in turmoil and the power of nature to heal even the most troubled hearts. Her characters are brave, flawed, real—at times disturbingly so—but she never gives up on any of them, and by the end of this inspiring novel, I shared her empathetic vision. A spare, commanding novel by a master storyteller."

—Patry Francis,
author of *The Orphans of Race Point*

"Lynne Hugo's writing is beautiful and evocative, earthy and strong. The characters, the setting, and the way she handles tough issues with honesty, grit, and understanding all make for a wonderful read."

—Laura Harrington,
author of *Alice Bliss*

"This book helps us to know that when life knocks us to our knees, it is possible to get up and 'walk on.'"

—Laura Munson,
author of *This Is Not the Story You Think It Is*

"A character in *Remember My Beauties* is fond of saying, 'Lotsa ways to be blind,' but this wonderful novel also shows us there are many ways to see—many ways to see love, for instance, or family or forgiveness. I'll be remembering the beauty of this novel for a long time to come."

—Katrina Kittle,
author of *The Blessings of the Animals*

This is a work of fiction. All characters are products of the author's imagination, and any resemblance to persons living or dead is entirely coincidental.

Published by Switchgrass Books, an imprint of Northern Illinois University Press
Northern Illinois University Press, DeKalb 60115
© 2016 by Northern Illinois University Press
Printed in the United States of America
25 24 23 22 21 20 19 18 17 16   1 2 3 4 5

978-0-87580-736-2 (paper)
978-1-60909-195-8 (ebook)

Book and cover design by Shaun Allshouse

Library of Congress Cataloging-in-Publication Data
Names: Hugo, Lynne, author.
Title: Remember my beauties / Lynne Hugo.
Description: DeKalb : Switchgrass Books, an imprint of Northern Illinois
    University Press, [2016]
Identifiers: LCCN 2016005087 (print) | LCCN 2016010348 (ebook) | ISBN
    9780875807362 (paperback) | ISBN 9781609091958 (electronic) | ISBN
    9781609091958 (Electronic)
Subjects: LCSH: Domestic fiction. | BISAC: FICTION / Literary. | FICTION /
    Family Life.
Classification: LCC PS3558.U395 R46 2016 (print) | LCC PS3558.U395 (ebook) |
    DDC 813/.54--dc23
LC record available at http://lccn.loc.gov/2016005087

REMEMBER

MY

BEAUTIES

Lynne Hugo

SWITCHGRASS BOOKS   NORTHERN ILLINOIS UNIVERSITY PRESS   DeKalb

Acknowledgments

As solitary a passion and occupation as writing is, we get by with a lot of help from our friends. Debra Connor and Nancy Pinard, my first readers, were extraordinarily generous with time and useful ideas. Janice Rockwell gave the manuscript several close reads for clarity, providing immeasurable assistance and support. Dawn Bordewisch served as an invaluable consultant regarding addiction treatment and recovery. Lucinda Dyer, author of *Back to Work: How to Rehabilitate or Recondition Your Horse,* read the manuscript and provided expert information and suggestions regarding horse care and riding, as well as directing me to specific articles by equine veterinarians. David A. Rockwell, MD, helped me with medical information regarding glaucoma and rheumatoid arthritis. Finally, Jodi Duff, DVM, read the manuscript and consulted with me regarding horse care and equine medicine. I am grateful beyond words to each of them.

The following books were read and/or consulted in the preparation of this work of fiction:

- *Horsewatching: Why Does a Horse Whinny and Everything Else You Ever Wanted to Know* by Desmond Morris (New York: Crown, 1989)
- *The Man Who Listens to Horses: The Story of a Real-Life Horse Whisperer* by Monty Roberts (New York: Ballantine Books, 1999)
- *Practical Horseman's Book of Horsekeeping* edited by M. A. Stoneridge (Garden City, NY: Doubleday, 1983)
- *The New Book of the Horse: Complete, Authoritative Reference for Every Horse Lover* by Sarah Haw (New York: Howell Book House, 1993)
- *Grassland: The History, Biology, Politics and Promise of the American Prairie* by Richard Manning (New York: Viking, 1995)

I also consulted the following websites and articles:

- HorseChannel.com, http://www.horsechannel.com
- "Tendon Injuries (Bowed Tendons) In Horses," James M. Casey, http://www.equinehorsevet.com
- "Bowed Tendons: The Farrier's Role in Prevention and Treatment," Heather Smith Thomas, November 1, 2012, http://www.americanfarriers.com/articles/506-bowed-tendons-the-farriers-role-in-prevention-and-treatment
- "Standing Wrap How-To," Laurie Pitts with Tricia Booker, *Practical Horseman Magazine,* February 2014, http://practicalhorsemanmag.com/article/standing-wrap-how-to-14725
- "Three Leg-Icing Techniques for Your Horse," Barb Crabbe, *Horse & Rider,* http://horseandrider.com/article/eqlegicing1818-17850

Managing Editor Nathan Holmes, Marketing Director Lori Propheter, and Art and Production Manager Shaun Allshouse at Northern Illinois University Press have been wonderfully caring and responsive. An author couldn't ask for better. Thanks also are due Director Linda Manning and Copyeditor Tracy Schoenle.

Special thanks again and always to Dr. Alan deCourcy for computer maintenance and rescue, which seems very important until I think of his constant faith, abiding love.

For Brooke
with my love

All the Queen's Horses

Twenty-six years since high school. My hair has been a long jungle of gold the whole time and it's not my hair that's wrong. Now kitchen shears are poised just above my forehead while I pull a fistful straight up from my scalp. My eyes glitter like river rocks in the bathroom mirror.

The hand with the scissors wears the engagement and wedding rings from Wal-Mart Supercenter's jewelry department. If you want, I tell myself, instead of cutting off your hair, you can take those off and drop them in the toilet. One half-carat total weight. Big deal. Who cares? Little glints around a fantasy. Little freaking glints. Big freaking fantasy.

But another divorce? The first one didn't help. I'm the ball in one of those arcade games, ratcheted and battered between my parents and my daughter, two consecutive husbands, and now stepchildren. Something else has to change. Something that will make people sit back, shut up, and see that I have to be different. To save myself.

For lack of a better plan, I let my hands have their way.

Bangs, hardly an inch long, jut a path across my forehead, and my hands keep clear-cutting the forest of my hair. It drops into the sink in hanks the color of fall leaves. Some miss and drift to the floor. Like a jerky chainsaw team, my hands cut down one side, then the other, over each ear, and halfway toward the back of my head.

It was my hair that Eddie fell in love with. At least at first. He always wanted me to let it loose when we made love, even if it got in our eyes and mouths. He'd wrap it around his hands and breathe in my scented shampoo and tell me it was beautiful, I was beautiful. Those were glory days of discovering all the treasure in each other that the world had carelessly overlooked. We were drunk on disbelief in our luck.

We've sobered up in five years. Now part of me lives here in our tri-level in town with the nice yard, with Eddie and his daughter, Chastity, an ironic name considering how she dresses—not that he sees it. The rest of me lives ten miles out on the farm with Mama and Daddy and the best, the remainder of our stable. Of all of them, the horses are the least trouble and wellspring of purest love. By pure, I mean uncomplicated.

I'd been ripe for the picking. Sure, I had great hair, but Eddie could have been smitten with my third toe and I'd probably have bought it. A year before I met him, my parents had started truly falling apart. I was living with Carley in an apartment on Marquette Drive in town. Carley's father had solved his child-support problem by disappearing when she was three. I managed with a Novocain-for-the-mind job: data entry in an insurance company cubicle. With morning and evening trips to the farm, I kept my parents fed, their house and laundry in order, and the horses cared for. There were a hundred problems popping up and taking over like weeds in the vegetable garden. A nursing home was the obvious answer.

"That's where you put people to die," Mama accused me. What I couldn't stand up to, though, were my father's wet eyes. "The horses . . ." he said. "What will happen to my beauties?" It wasn't a question but a moan of resignation and heartbreak.

How could he say such a thing to me? The horses are our connection: the corral, ring, and pastures our idea of an open cathedral, time with the horses our version of *where two or three are gathered together*. We've had the same experience—oh I know it used to happen to him, too—seeing the horses come in from the back pasture on their own even before I call, how caring for them in the dawns and twilights can feel mysterious and reciprocal, a sense that whatever life means, all that lives are in it together.

"Daddy, I would always keep the horses. They're everything to me. For heaven's sake, *I* bought Spice. He's mine. But I love them all. You know that."

"Okay" was his word at the same time he shook his head. No comfort on his face. I've never given him cause to wonder how much I love the horses, except that unlike him, I don't put them before my family, regardless of what Eddie thinks. I'd have to do it all, or my father would never be peaceful.

"Don't worry," I said. "You know what? I'll keep you and Mama and the horses here at home. Carley and I will move in with you." I'd always intended to keep the horses, barn, and pastures; my idea was for Daddy and Mama to rent out the house for income. The whole part about moving in to take care of them was impulse pure as honey and disaster thick as the same.

I did it, though, and it wasn't the first nor the last dumb thing I've done for lack of a better alternative when I couldn't stand the status quo any more. Carley sulked and glowered and made it clear that she'd rather bathe in horse pee than help. I set up our own apartment in the basement, which she called the bat cave.

"Give it a rest, Carley. There are no bats in the basement," I said.

She reached for her purse and took out a small mirror, shoving it toward my face. "Take a look."

Her real name is Carla Rose, and she hasn't gone to charm school in the intervening years. But while she and I were living with Mama and Daddy, I could still harangue her off to seventh and then eighth grade. I'd get up early for our morning fight and fix breakfast, then arrange Mama and Daddy's lunch and lay out their pills like little soldiers for the day. Tired before I'd even showered, remembered or forgotten a smack of lipstick, I sped to the office chronically a few minutes late. I lived for the sweet seasons when I could turn the horses out to pasture—no stalls to muck, no extra time allotted to throwing hay, scooping grain—and I could work each horse under saddle every day. For pleasure I'd ride bareback.

It was Eddie's asking to come over to watch me ride that made me fall in love with him. He said the way I knew everything about horses was amazing, and his eyes adored me from under his thick brows and buzz cut. So I showed off a little. Instead of the jeans and the Western boots I'd taken to wearing, which were practical for barn work, I dug out the breeches and tall boots I'd kept from back when Charyzma and I competed in hunter classes. Carley must have appropriated my jacket and gloves, but I found the white show shirt and my helmet, and for all Eddie knew, the outfit was right. I set up a cavalletti and a low bar in the ring, first trotting Charyzma over the cavalletti and then, when she was happy doing that, cantering her around and asking her to jump the bar, which I set at two feet, not daring anything higher since I hadn't kept up her jumps. I should have made the time. I could have set that bar at four feet, Charyzma had that much room to spare. She wanted to jump again, and so did I. Eddie inspired me. Back then, he cared about my Carley, too, although an irritated skunk would have given him a more pleasant reception. He said it was shameful how her father had deserted her, that he'd never do that. He was crazy about his own children, a true sign of a good man. The hole I'd dug for myself over Carley having no father, Eddie was there to fill. I admit there was exquisite electricity between us, and it was the first time I understood lust, but I trusted him, too.

When I told Carley that Eddie and I loved each other and wanted to make plans, she ramped up her opposition until it was a force of nature.

"You cannot marry that dork," she yelled. "He wears overalls. He wears white socks and *black shoes*. I hate him. He hates me. I hate his stupid daughter. Chastity's a slut."

I couldn't argue her last point or Eddie's idea of dress attire. "Chassie's only with him every other weekend. And Eddie does not hate you. He wants to love you and for us all to be a family." I didn't even bother to mention Rocky, Eddie's third-grade son, because his ex-wife hardly ever let him come, always in some new uproar about child support, or she'd claim Rocky had Ebola and was representing Brazil in an ice hockey tournament, both the same weekend. "And here's the thing, Carley. Eddie and I figure we can buy a house with both our incomes. You won't have to live in the 'bat cave' anymore." I put air quotes around bat cave but softened it with a smile. I can't say the smile was entirely genuine, but I was trying. I thought she was just being fourteen, that special nastiness they save for their mothers. I hadn't figured out that she was cutting school and forging my name on the excuse notes, or swiping money from my purse and her blind grandfather's sock drawer.

She and I were in the basement at the time, my parents upstairs, doubtless eavesdropping on every word through the register, though I kept a hush on. I'd fashioned a nice place for us down there. A blue couch on a beige carpet remnant, a coffee table, and two end tables with lamps. Our own TV. Bright red-and-blue tapestry on the wall to hide painted cinder blocks. Silk plants, some red candles. A refrigerator and a microwave against the far back wall. The one separate room was Carley's. An unused desk with good lighting, carpet littered with her clothing, a twin bed rumpled with pillows and comforter. There wasn't much natural light, but we did have privacy. Still, Carley did nothing but complain as if she were being paid by the word.

But then, her neck reddening, she said, "And who's gonna take care of Grandma and Grandpa? What about the *horses*? I wanna stay here."

She was a pretty girl back then—still is, if you can get beyond the piercings, which were just for normal earrings at first. Now, barely six years later, it's up to twelve in her left ear, seven in her right, and a new horror in her right eyebrow. To my mind, she looks like the victim of a nail-gun assault. And she's taken to dyeing her blond hair black, which makes her fair skin look ghostly and cloudlike. She's not yet found a way to mess up her eyes—big, and a good sky blue like mine—except to imitate a raccoon, courtesy of white eye shadow, black liner, and mascara applied to full theatrical effect.

My plan was to stay calmly rational with Carley while explaining the arrangements. Eddie and I had discussed it and been delusional enough to believe that would be effective. "They qualify for County Eldercare Health Services," I said. "They'll have an aide here four hours, every day. Meals on Wheels, too. I'm keeping them on that. I'll come before work to give them breakfast and their morning pills, and Meals on Wheels will provide dinners. So I'll be checking on them and taking care of the horses, of course, and Nadine says she'll help with Grandma and Grandpa, too," I said, knowing full well that the last was laughable but feeling the need for one more item to pile on the excellence of this plan.

"Oh *right*. Aunt Nadine. She won some daughter of the year award recently, didn't she? She'll be fan-*tastic*. So you'll be *doing it* with your new lover while some country strangers are taking care of Grandma and Grandpa?"

"That's *county*. *County* Eldercare Health Services. Your concern for your grandparents is touching. I just don't know how I could get by without all *your* help." I've never charged for sarcasm since it comes to me so naturally.

My calm and rational approach was derailing; I tried to fix it. "Baby, come here." I opened my arms. "I didn't mean that." I wanted to cradle her the way I used to when problems required a Band-Aid and a Popsicle, when fun was blowing dandelion fluff around a melon sunset, making firefly lanterns, and driving into town for ice cream. I so miss how she loved me.

"Let go, honey," Eddie always says to me. "Kids change." But I'll never stop hoping to get her back. I taught her to ride before she was old enough to start in 4-H. She has the gift. When she was eight, Carley raised Charyzma's foal. She showed him for four years at the Kentucky State Fair. Her bulletin board spilled first- and second-place ribbons. Pot and cocaine never occurred to me while trophies were lining up like a shiny cavalry on her dresser.

"You don't give a shit about anything but yourself," she sneered, pulling out of my reach. "You just can't wait to shack up with that asshole."

She might as well have been a stinging wasp, and my urge to slap was just as reflexive and wrongheaded. But that's what I did. I don't think I slapped her hard. It takes thought to wind up and put power in a slap. But I saw her pause and take the time to decide: yes, she would. She drew back to hit me. What had begun as a skid out of control was dropping into slow motion, something dangerous that wouldn't be excusable as impulse.

I shouted, "Don't you dare!" She dared. I grabbed her wrist, staggering backward under the force of her thrust. I went down, half over the coffee table, half onto the floor, between it and the couch, pulling Carley on top of me. That was an accident; I'd grabbed her wrist to save myself.

The table skittered to one side, and the couch jarred enough to knock over the ginger-jar lamp, which shattered on the cement floor. Carley screamed and started flailing, arms and legs like a windmill pummeling me.

"Let me up! Stop!" I gasped, trying to free my arms to push her off me.

Three things happened: her elbow caught me in the throat, her weight started to suffocate me, and the door at the top of the stairs opened.

"What's going on down there?" Daddy called.

My only thought was to keep him from coming down. "It's okay, Daddy. Everything's fine. Just close the door." But I couldn't get enough air, so I was rasping.

Carley shouted, "Grandpa, she's fucking trying to kill me," while she thrashed, her voice trumping mine.

Daddy didn't hesitate a beat. "Don't know what took her so long. I'd a done it last year." He slammed the door.

At that Carley went rigid as a death wish. Then the fight leaked out of her. She tried to climb off me, but her limbs hadn't the will to work.

She was crying. I got my palms on the floor and managed to leverage myself to a sitting position, which bumped Carley down into my lap. I stroked her head and worked my arms under and around her. My hair fell forward over my shoulders like a blanket over the two of us, and I let it be. Carley, my baby, my beauty.

"Oh sweetheart, he didn't mean that. He didn't mean it." My mouth tasted like bad milk around the lie. My father has never said such a thing to anyone. Mama's the bigmouth.

"He hates me," she sobbed. "I didn't know. I thought Grandpa loved me, he let me train Charyzma's foal."

"He doesn't hate you, honey. The foal was a long time ago. He may be tired of back talk or he may be tired of you not helping now, but that's different from hate."

Carley was having none of it. She raised her head from my lap, face smeared, eyes and nose running. "He hates me and I don't want to stay here anymore."

"What do you want to do? You don't want me to marry Eddie and move, but you don't want to stay here."

"I don't care. Go ahead. Marry Eddie if it'll get us the hell out of here."

There were twenty smart things I could have said and another twenty I could have done. But I was so tired, and this seemed like a crazy wedding gift from Daddy. I'm ashamed to say I accepted it. I thought Eddie would help me change Carley's life, even though she was too young and dumb to know it.

"All right, honey. I'll marry Eddie and we'll move out of here. We'll get a new start."

I meet my own eyes in the mirror. I've cut almost the front half of my hair. Now that the wild flourish that usually falls around my face has been hacked away, I see old-lady lines around my eyes. I hardly recognize myself. A fragment from a song I used to know comes to me. "Wasted on the Way." If that isn't the title, it should be, at least for my life. If I could remember the words, maybe I'd know what to do. It was something like . . . *I should've started long ago.* . . . I look around the bathroom in that way you do, idly, when you're just trying to remember something. I see the toilet seat. Up. Again.

That's it: the words are about water. Water . . . or time . . . going under a bridge. I wait, trying to retrieve it. And then I start to hear the song from somewhere in my lost self: *let water carry it away.* So I take another hank of the hair Eddie loves, saw it off, and drop it into the yawning mouth of the toilet. I've started to hum the melody, enjoying my work, when I hear Eddie tromping upstairs and down the hallway toward our bedroom. Our beagle runs ahead to see what's going on in the bathroom just as I shut the door to hide what my hands are doing. The door hits Copper on the side of the head. He yelps, and I have to open it to make sure he's all right.

"Holy shit!" Eddie gapes at the hair on the floor, on the sink, on my shoulders, and my half-cut head. "What the hell are you doing? Oh no, no! What are you *doing*? You *can't* cut off your *hair.* You *promised.*"

He sinks to his knees, frantically gathering what's fallen, looks up at me, pleading, raising the fallen hair like a prayer in his two hands. Tears in his eyes. "I'm sorry, I'm sorry. Please stop. *Please.* Can you put it back? You know, like make those extension things with it? Those things Chassie wants? I'm sorry, I'm *sorry.*"

Eddie stayed on his knees in the bathroom pleading apologies until Jewel's fit passed and she put the scissors down.

"Oh my God, are you nuts?" he said then, standing and brushing hair from his pants. His voice rose, upset. "Have you gone lunatic crazy?" The dog started barking, as he did when anyone got loud. His wife's face told him that he wasn't being supportive, like she'd told him a thousand times he needed to be. He tried again. "I mean, you can fix this, can't you?"

Jewel picked up the scissors. "Wait, honey," he said. "Maybe that didn't come out right. I'm sorry."

Jewel sighed as if she was giving up but kept her grip on the scissors. "Eddie, I can't fight with you anymore. I just can't. It's *my* hair, she's *my* daughter, they're *my* horses. It's all the same difference." She was looking at herself in the mirror, not at him.

Eddie was baffled until he remembered that they'd been arguing. What was it about? The checkbook was low. He'd said she should quit buying Carley food 'cause it just supports her habit—something like that? She said it's more important than Chassie's acrylic nails. Jesus, what else did he say? It's a money-sucking waste to keep the horses? Yeah, okay. But not a word about her hair. "Carley? The horses? Is that why you"—don't step on a land mine—"did this?"

She spoke slowly, like he was the demented one. "I'm a person, Eddie. I'm doing what *I* decide, not you. Can you grasp that?"

The glare of the bathroom lights over the mirror was hurting his eyes and making it hard to see her face well. She'd been at her folks' house with the horses earlier and was still in her barn clothes; a faint horsey smell came from her jeans. They always ate dinner late because Jewel took care of her parents and the horses on her way home from work. It hadn't started out that way. When they got married, Jewel was supposed to just take care of the horses, but Jewel's mother had fussed about and with each aide the county agency sent in, and Jewel had ended up having to do the work anyway. Finally she'd figured she might as well get the pay for it. So she'd gotten certified, and now it brought in a sweet extra sum, enough that they'd bought a nicer house. When Chassie wanted to move in, they'd had the space. Jewel had been dead against it—claimed it wasn't fair since he wouldn't let Carley live with them anymore—but he'd argued that his daughter was no druggie and therefore a different case entirely.

Not that he really believed tough love was going to change Carley's drug habits: the truth he didn't want to tell Jewel was that he just yearned for a normal life, and he didn't think druggies were any more likely to change than nutcases like his ex. Jewel ought to look at her crackhead sister, Nadine, for one example. Whatever. It all seemed fairly black and white to him, in addition to the true fact that the horses took up a ton of time that Jewel could be at home, and she was spending a bunch of money on them, too. His eyes worked just fine on the checkbook deductions and balance.

"Do you *get* it?" Jewel said, and he saw that she'd rotated the scissors so the point was toward him. He didn't know that he understood or didn't; he wasn't sure what she was talking about. He was dumbfounded by what she'd done to her hair and by the shears aimed at his gut. He wondered if she was high. He'd never known her to use anything.

"Yes, yes, honey, I understand," he lied softly. "I understand. Please, just put the scissors down."

He led Jewel's gaze with his own to her hand, pulled her eyes down deliberately, watched her realize what he meant her to see. When she did, he saw that she was startled, and she laid the scissors on the bathroom counter. Finally he was getting her on track. Now Eddie tried to lead her eyes to the mirror so she would see what she'd done to her hair. No luck this time. She brushed past him out of the bathroom without a word, Copper at her heels.

Eddie started to follow but thought better of it when she slammed the bedroom door right as Copper's tail cleared it. This wasn't like his Jewel, not at all. He turned and took the five steps back to the hallway bathroom—she'd not used the one off their bedroom—and surveyed the proof of insanity lying on the counter and floor and in the toilet. The place looked like a salon that hadn't been swept in two days. On his knees again, Eddie picked up the clumps he'd already held and dropped, and as much as he could of the rest of it, gathering and arranging the strands in his big left hand. When they made love he'd wrap his hands in this very hair and nuzzle into Jewel's neck for the smell of it, like fruit. It was her, his wife, and he wanted to breathe her in and in and in. Before they'd married, she'd promised him she wouldn't cut her hair. She'd promised.

Eddie had two dead parents, two child support payments (even though he had one of the children himself), a for-shit job in a mill, and an ex-wife who was a mutant cross between a bitter bitch and a dangerous whack job. ("Bipolar disorder," according to Chassie, which Eddie considered just another piece of crap excuse. Chassie said her mother wouldn't take the medication. Eddie said, "Well, your mother is more than one sandwich short of a picnic." Chassie got huffy then, but the truth was that even Chassie avoided Lana when she could get away with it.) Jewel was, well, of course he loved her, but more: Jewel was Eddie's heart, his *good*. He had Jewel and because of Jewel, he had Chassie and the means and place to have his son, Rocky, who was now saying he wanted to come live with them, a little fact Eddie hadn't sprung on Jewel yet. Jewel couldn't be going all crazy on him now.

He left her alone, figuring that was temporarily safest, while he headed for the kitchen, lifted a beer from the refrigerator as quietly as he could, opened the can, and pondered a course of action. He tried to keep his mind off her hair, which he'd carried down the half flight of their tri-level, rested momentarily on the breakfast bar while he fetched the beer, and hunted an envelope in the built-in desk. The wallpaper behind it was red with a weird yellow scroll thing at the top. He'd disliked it when Jewel picked it out, and tonight it struck him as nuts. A white business envelope wasn't nearly big enough for all the hair, which broke his heart again. "All the king's horses and all the king's men couldn't put Jewel together again," he whispered and, suddenly broken himself, gave way to tears.

He'd never made it past the family room couch, the blue one that Jewel had moved from the basement apartment at her parents' house. By the time he woke in the morning, too many crushed beer cans on the table, the light in the room told him it was mid-morning. It was Saturday: Jewel would have left for her parents' place by seven.

The small herd was grazing near the larger pond, which was in the far back pasture. April bluegrass was longest where the pond was spring-fed, although both pastures were glorious, surrounded by white Kentucky board fencing. The horses' ears flicked occasionally toward the quiet road, out of sight. Any sound might be Her. They used to start moving to the front pasture toward the corral anytime they heard The Noise—like many, many hooves on gravel—right by the house, but Spice, a black Arab gelding, learned to differentiate. Now they waited for Spice to know if it was Her before they started toward the barn, even though Charyzma, a bay Thoroughbred, was the dominant mare and claimed the lead.

Spice raised his head, ears forward. The Right Sound. Now, walk on. When She called, lilting the sounds to summon them on the breeze, they would already be most of the way to Her. She'd start calling anyway, and She'd be carrying some apples or carrots. Sugar lumps. Sometimes Red, a roan Quarter Horse gelding, or Moonbeam, a white and black Appaloosa mare, would try to be first, which Charyzma would or wouldn't bother to correct, but Spice didn't care. She always slipped him an extra sugar when She was brushing him down or after She cleaned his feet. Sometimes a stone would be lodged in one hoof, up against the tender frog, and he understood what She did for him when She picked it out or removed burrs from his coat. So when She arrived, he nickered his happiness, and when She hugged his neck and kissed his face, he nuzzled Her. Sometimes when She came, She'd cling to each of them a long time. If it was warm, She might soak them with water and scrub a new scent onto them, then more water and a good rub with cloth, and finally brushing. She'd stay while the sun slid across the sky, and She'd ride each of them, maybe bareback, maybe under saddle. Spice was patient by nature, even when he and two others were waiting in the paddock while She took Charyzma in the ring to work her and then Moonbeam. Charyzma didn't like to be separated from Moonie. But She knew about this and kept them from each other's sight when She exercised those two. Of course She knew. She'd been there through every season since they had been colts and fillies.

She talked to them all always, and always, before She left, Her arms would be around each of their necks again, Her face against theirs, stroking them, each in turn. To make Her sound like the creek down in the woods when it played so light and easy with the rocks, Spice would nod his head softly against Hers when She put Her face on his to talk to him. He was always last before She left, and always She left with the sides of Her mouth turned up. He knew Her, too.

I Am, I Said

"GOD IN HEAVEN, WHAT happened? You're gonna sue, right?" Mama says when I arrive to fix their breakfast.

She propels her wheelchair toward my shins as I clear the front door. She's dressed herself, I'm glad to see, though her shirt, a big neon pink flower print, hurts my eyes. Through the open doorway, I glimpse Daddy in his easy chair. He's dressed too, his cane propped exactly where it belongs, between his right leg and where his hand rests on the arm of the chair. He turns toward our voices.

"What's the matter? Sue who?" he calls in without getting up.

"Sue her hairdresser," Mama says, staring, trying to work her blowsy face from horror toward sympathy. Her own hair is no masterpiece, looking like a storm cloud chock-full of summer hail. Jowly and flushed with high blood pressure, Mama never looks well. Her brows are thin and pale, and her teeth have gone grayish-yellow. Her eyes, though, are mine, which scares me.

"Her hairdresser's named Sue?" Daddy says. "Why do we care what her hairdresser calls herself?"

"Sheesh, Hack, I'm talking 'bout Jewel suing her hairdresser. She's come in here with a haircut to make sweet Jesus weep. Front and sides all cut off like a man's. Back's in a ponytail."

Daddy clears his throat, not one to comment on women's hairstyles. Or perhaps he's wondering what his hair looks like, considering that I'm the one who cuts it. After I scissor the top, I always use the clippers on the sides and back. "Lean forward, Daddy. Now to the right. A little more," I'll say as I guide his head with my hand. Then I trim his eyebrows and go over his face and neck with the electric shaver, erasing the fine growth that's appeared. When I'm undoing the homemade plastic cape from the back of his neck, he'll sometimes reach back and catch my hand to hold it against his cheek. *Thank you*, he might whisper, and if he does I lean in to kiss the air by his cheek.

If he could see himself, he wouldn't find the mirror mean. His hair is a neat thatch of coarse iron over a broad face with earthy eyes, hawkish nose, faint beard, small mouth. What *is* remarkable is how unwrinkled he remains, how compact his body still is. His grandfather was half Cherokee; his grandmother just an Appalachian, he says, a blue-eyed woman with farm-roughened hands. I can see a bit of the Indian in him but not in myself.

Mama took care of Daddy when he first went blind from glaucoma. Meanwhile, she went from a cane to a walker, her legs ruined by rheumatoid arthritis. He tried to take over when she first needed a wheelchair. The blind led the lame and vice versa. Mama would direct Daddy in the dark kitchen at the back of the house, where threadbare plaid dish towels languished, then as now, next to faded print place mats. "The soup's in the cupboard to the left side of the sink. No, no, the other left side. Good. No, I'm tired of tomato. Jewel's gotta quit buying that all the time. Pull out another can. Okay, beef noodle. Now, the opener is three steps to the right. Pull it to the edge of the counter for me."

"Did some sicko do this to you in your sleep?" Mama says.

Here we go, I think, opening my mouth to shoot a sarcastic bullet, but her face looks strange. I stop myself and walk to where she's parked, staring at me.

"Can we quit on the subject of my hair?" I say and try my best diversionary shot. "Here, I brought you donuts. It's a gorgeous day. I'm opening the windows. The lilies of the valley haven't quite finished, and you'll be able to smell them."

When I was young, Mama always insisted my curly hair be cut boyishly close around my head, though the fashion was long, and I wanted to look like the other girls. "You won't take care of it," she said. She meant she had too much else for me to do to let me take the time to fuss with myself. The dubious reward of growing it out after I turned eighteen was that both my first and second husbands fell in love with my hair. No danger of that happening now; a man would have to be as blind as my father. I risked one glance in the mirror when I brushed my teeth, and it was all I could stand. I thought it might not be so noticeable if I put what's left in a ponytail, so without looking, I pulled it through a rubber band. Obviously, I haven't hidden a thing.

"Oh damn. Oh, Mama." She's crying. I lean over and gather her in my arms.

"Who did this to you?" she says, struggling to get her hands up to the sides of my head. I twist my neck to avoid the contact.

"Nobody, Mama. I did it myself."

"I don't believe you." She's sniffling, face pressed on my chest like an oversized peony. I'm bent at an awkward angle, and my back hurts, but I keep squatting and holding her while she cries. "You're protecting somebody. Eddie didn't do this. He loves your hair. Wasn't Carley, was it?"

"Mama, I'm always protecting somebody. Except this time." I smooth her hair back from her forehead.

She uses the rare moment that I feel tender for her. "Your brother's coming home t' see us. It'll be—"

I jerk away, and Mama's head bounces.

"No. No way. No way Cal is coming in this house. Not while I'm doing the work here. No." I say as I unfold, and then I'm fully upright, towering over her. I'm not shouting, but my voice is loud. I'm five-nine barefoot, over five-ten in my boots, and willing to put every inch and decibel on the line right now to stop this.

"What's going on in there?" Daddy calls, turning his head toward us. I can see him through the hallway that leads into the scrubby living room.

"Nothing," Mama calls back. "Just talking 'bout her hair, that's all."

"Daddy! Do you know about this? About Cal coming back here?" He doesn't answer, which is answer enough.

"Daddy? . . . Daddy!"

No answer.

Too stung, I don't go in to challenge him. Instead, I aim at Mama. "I moved in to take care of you after he got in trouble—again. He ran off—again. What has *he* done for you?" I feel my face reddening in anger. Cal used to tease me without mercy about it.

"Oh here she goes," Mama says, switching from pitiful to disdainful. "Seems to me you moved back out when it suited you. What's the difference? Cal's got his life to live."

"That's the point. I haven't gotten to live mine. I've been taking care of people, including the two of you. Or haven't you noticed I'm here twice a day?" I start to go on but feel tears coming up behind my eyes and harden my face against them. "I'm going to the barn now."

"Daddy's hungry," Mama says to my back.

"Guess you should have waited to mention Cal till after your faces were fed then." From the refrigerator, I take four big carrots, their long green graduation tassels flopping, stuff my shirt pocket with sugar lumps, and let the screen door slap shut behind me. Daddy can find cold cereal to tide him over. Mama is likely talking about herself. They're both wanting the hot breakfast I cook them on weekend mornings: pancakes and sausage or bacon and eggs and hot muffins. Those nights I cook a full dinner, too, everything they like from the old times. Tonight they'd been going to get chicken and dumplings.

Once I am outdoors in the rinsed-off sunlight, I stand and breathe in, breathe out, trying to slow my heart. My father won't stand up for me, but for him I regularly give up the time I might have for myself to put him on Moonbeam. I ride Spice and use a lead rope to pony them down an easy trail over the creek crossing and back, talking all the way, telling Daddy exactly where we are on his own land and what it looks like. Lately he wants to hear about the soft magenta bloom of the henbit and the school-bus yellow of the black mustard in the pasture before he asks me, *what about the nettle,* and I have to say, *yes, it's been as purple as ever this spring, yes, the color of that awful Easter hat Mama had back in '71,* and he laughs the way he always does and reminds me that's why he really went blind. He listens for the bluebirds and chuck-will's-widow's mating calls, then nods as hoof sounds change from bluegrass pasture to soft dirt to clanging on stones. He discerns the amount of water in the wide creek by its rush or trickle, how his horse moves through it. There is light in his eyes, almost as if he can see the cattailed ponds and open sky of our pastures, the stippled forest trail, the great blue heron we startle up over the singing little river. I could trot, canter, let Spice gallop the open pasture like the Arab he is, instead of staying in a slow walk, but for my father I try to forget how perfectly I can make my body move in concert with my horse. I even give up paying attention to the feel of the reins, the smell of neat's-foot oil lingering on the saddle, to focus completely on him. In the saddle my father recognizes himself, and, yes, now that he needs me, he thanks me out loud. But he won't do what would count: he won't stand up for me. The tack room is at the very end of the barn; it used to be the barn's business office, too, when I was a kid. I open the outside door and, without entering, pull a hoof pick and a curry brush off the tool shelf, and one halter from a hook, then go through the corral and front pasture gate and start walking. Good, loyal friends, all four horses are already over the rise. Charyzma, as usual, is a few steps in the lead. She's Daddy's tall bay Thoroughbred mare, a beautiful jumper although Daddy had hoped for more speed back when she was his last best hope as a breeder. When I see them, I can't hold tears in.

"Hey, my boy. Hey, good girl. I'm sorry. No grain today. I've got carrots, though. Here you go, baby," I say, feeding each of them. Spice wants Moonbeam's. Moonie is Daddy's sweetheart. I think the black spots dappling her white coat were one of the last things he could distinguish. Or wanted to. "Hey, back off, you had yours," I whisper, nuzzling my face against Spice's. Not that he holds his head still for long; they rarely do. Instead he searches my shirt pocket for sugar. Charyzma shows more patience than I'd ever expect of a Thoroughbred. She lowers her long neck for the last carrot. She has a soft mouth. I think of how Daddy never used anything but a rubber D-ring snaffle bit on her, but that was his favorite anyway because rubber is softer than metal, and the joint in the center keeps pressure off the horse's tongue. Daddy never believed in pain or fear as the way to train a horse. His time and kindness were what they got from him, no matter how much rearing or bucking a skittish colt did at first. Of course I was jealous.

Now I slide the halter on Red, a smart, bombproof red roan Quarter Horse, a sixteen-hand gelding with a white blaze and socks. I brush him thoroughly—which I'll do to all the horses as a way of checking them over and loving their whole selves—then lift the first hoof by running my hand down Red's cannon and tapping his fetlock lightly and saying, "Give me your foot." Old images come to me as if a tumbler of time has been upended. I balance each of

Red's hooves on my thigh in turn. Use the pick to clean around the shoe to the bars, sole, and frog, get out whatever he's got stuck in there. Packed manure, glass, a stone: any of it can make a horse go lame. I cry over what's stuck in me for which there is no pick. If you look up *trouble* in my dictionary, it will say, "Cause of misery. Synonym: Calvin."

From the time we were growing up, Cal has had Mama bamboozled. I can't remember a time he didn't light her face with his handsome smile and lie so convincingly that Jesus would have taken down his every word as gospel. Then out the door he'd go with his pals while Mama would plop herself in front of the TV and complain. "Jewel, I'm so tired. You see to the kitchen and get the laundry put up." Or she'd head to the bar after Daddy and drag his butt home but not before she'd had herself a couple. Not that she ever drank the way he did and not that it kept her from complaining about how he put it away.

It was no secret Cal was her favorite child. Daddy didn't play favorites, though that was possibly because he didn't pay attention enough to have one.

"Okay, boy, okay. Wait your turn," I say, scrubbing Spice's forehead where he likes to be scratched. He's a bit over fifteen hands, a registered half Arab (the other half is Quarter Horse), a gelding, all black. He has the calm gentleness of a Quarter Horse, yet the short back conformation and dished nose of an Arab. And the big eyes. A quick study, what makes him unique and beloved to my heart is how hard he works to please me; he's all mine and he knows it. I always slip him something extra. But he's a horse, not a child, and I truly love the others, too.

The older we got, the worse it got. I worked with Daddy in the barn as much as I could, because he'd occasionally say something to Cal like *Oh lay off the girl, you're giving me a headache* before he turned his mind back to the horses, and then Cal would flick me with a finger but quiet down. Cal's friends wore their hair in duck-tails and rolled cigarettes into their T-shirt sleeves. They got girls to go to second and third base. Home runs gave them bragging rights all over school. This took each girl by outraged surprise since the boys swore faithfulness and secrecy. I was all height and knees, with the fashion sense and budget of a land snail, so I didn't worry much about being their target. I'd found a way to be happy: the horses. We had six back then. They were the horses I learned with—how to saddle break even terrified green colts like a horse whisperer—with kindness. Daddy taught me, and those days I felt like I had a real parent. He saw I had the gift; it was my one claim to his pride and signs of affection. I drank coffee with him in the tack room through summer mornings. There was always a pot going there: strong, bitter, burned-tasting. He kept the radio on a country station, and we both wore Western hats and boots around the barn. An aging professionally painted sign over the tack room door read:

HACK'S STABLE
THOROUGHBRED BREEDING, TRAINING
LESSONS, GUIDED TRAIL RIDES
ENGLISH AND WESTERN PLEASURE

Daddy saw a way for me to bring money into the family, so he bought a couple of school horses. He wanted me to give lessons to children. Then, when Daddy turned the most of the business over to me, I was the one to take customers out on guided trail rides. That meant more income to the stable. I guess that by then it had started occurring to Daddy that his dream of really making it as a Thoroughbred trainer was headed for an early death. Or it didn't. He never said, but by then there were rarely more than one or two horses he was training for other people at our farm—just enough that he could teach me what he knew. He knew everything but how to stop. I got pretty good at covering for him, but Daddy's drinking likely messed with his reputation.

By the time I was slowly taking over, our Thoroughbred breeding was down to what came out of one mare, Hannah's Fine Ride. Hannah was by Fritz 'n' Thunder, who'd missed taking the Preakness by a nose; Charyzma was her foal, born after I got married the first time. Daddy kept Charyzma, convinced she could produce champions down the road, that's how perfect she was. Maybe she's a little nervous, but Thoroughbreds are like that. She was lamb-gentle, just easily spooked, like her mother. Daddy had only been able to get

Hannah because she'd been injured during training for the Derby as a three-year-old and was unfit to race.

Cal was supposed to muck the stalls, but he'd have left the horses in shit up to their chests and found a way to get away with it. I did it, and spent hours braiding their manes and tails, an excuse to stay with them longer. Right now I braid Spice's tail, slowly, combing and dividing the sections over and over as if they were past, present, and future and I could weave them together in some coherent way.

I had reason to dislike Cal. Even hate him. I kept clear of him, enough that I didn't know he was messing with drugs. If I'd paid attention, I could have figured it out. The truth is, I did everything I could to avoid him.

Until he came into my room when I was asleep. He was drunk and he was high. He'd closed the door to keep the darkness in; my shades were down. He said nothing. I fought, first to consciousness, then to make my arms and legs thrash, as if terror were water and I was drowning. *Swim, swim, fight, breathe, scream.* I opened my mouth, sucked in air to scream. The weight of his hand moved from where it was squeezing my breast and clamped over my mouth. His other hand was pulling my nightgown up. His knee forced my legs apart amid a chaotic tangle of sheet and struggle.

Spice twists his head as I comb his mane. "I'm sorry. I didn't mean to hurt you. Good boy, good boy," I say, even though I know he's just getting impatient with being fussed over. But I'm remembering how *I* twisted my head, and though Cal clamped down, his hand slipped, and I had a chance. I jerked up enough to bite down with all my strength on the web of his thumb. And I didn't let go. He yelled, and it was then that I knew it was Cal. I still didn't let go. I tasted his blood. Cal was the one who lost that time. He was just over seventeen. I was sixteen. Nadine would have been eight.

"If you don't want anybody in your room, lock your door. Don't blame Cal if he has a couple and gets confused where he is. Grow up, girl," Mama interrupted me when I told her he'd been high and came into my room. "You stay here and watch Nadine. I'm goin' up to fetch your father b'fore he can't find his way home." I argued back, trying to tell her the rest. Suddenly she shut her eyes, tears leaking out from under the lids, and, like a child, she stuck her fingers in her ears.

"Cal's a good boy, Jewel. He's a *good boy*, a good boy." It was nearly a chant. She was begging me. The knowledge would either destroy her or she'd make it my fault and destroy me. How could I go on? I stopped.

When I come back in the house, the happiness the horses give me doesn't last this time. I scarcely speak to Mama and Daddy while I cook their breakfast, vacuum, change the bed linens, and start the laundry. Yet I've calmed myself with the horses' sheer great *being*, which is a presence difficult to explain. I talk to them, and they pay complete attention at the same time they pay none at all, if that makes any sense, which I don't suppose it does. It's as I imagine God. They look at me the same way whether I've been a fine human being or petty and angry that day. Nothing interferes with being accepted into the purity and stillness that hovers around them. There's a great comfort in it.

"I'll be back to fix dinner," I say as I get ready to leave. There's no cheer in my voice, but I'm not surly either. Daddy's back in his chair, where he'll be until Mama gets out the lunch I've arranged for them on the center shelf of the refrigerator where it's easy for her to reach. Balogna and lettuce sandwiches wrapped in plastic, chips already on the table, plates and napkins laid out. Daddy can reach the ice with Mama directing him, and she can open their Cokes. During the day, Mama gets herself on the toilet with the help of the handrails installed on the walls of the bathroom. She claims their functioning is due to help from her collection of angels arranged all around the living room, including the top of the television, which is always on. I want to smash them, those guardian angels, fakes, every last one of them.

"We need lightbulbs," Daddy says.

"Says the blind man," I mutter under my breath. "Otherwise you might not be able to see where you left the car keys. Or have trouble finding the door to let Cal in." Aloud I say, "Okay, I'll put lightbulbs on the list. Anything else . . . *Mama?*"

"Don't need lightbulbs. Gettin' low on deodorant," she says.

"Okay."

This is no traditional Kentucky farmhouse. It's an old undistinguished ranch-style house. The furnishings are getting threadbare,
the decor was tacky to begin with, and now it practically shouts its
age: where there's carpet, it's olive shag; where there's flooring, it's
tan linoleum, cracked and sad. I'm standing at the door looking
back into the living room at Daddy who is staring at the television,
and I'm thinking how senseless and stupid it all is: a blind man
ordering lightbulbs and watching television. I'm thinking about
how Cal can just decide to show up after all these years, and Mama
will wheel right on over to make room for him. I close my eyes a
moment. Then I walk into the living room, turn off the television,
and plant myself in front of it. Daddy objects, and Mama swings
around to see what's going on. Before either can get going, I say,
softly, "Listen, both of you. Consider this business with Cal, because
I mean it. If you let him stay here, I'll quit. I may not have finished
cutting my hair, but I *will* finish this."

Then I turn the television back on and go out the front door into
the noon sun, my car keys jangling from my hand like they're my
every nerve.

Eddie and I are sitting outside on our patio after I've cooked dinner for Mama and Daddy over there and again here for us. Eddie's
probably thinking I should be grateful because he grilled the meat
and carried dishes. Big deal. Right now, he should be grateful I am
unarmed.

"Jewel, what has come over you?" he says after I tell him about
Cal coming back and my threat to quit. "First the hair and now this.
Maybe we should get you to a doctor, honey. I mean, maybe you
need some of that medicine they give people when their mind sort
of goes south. You know—a breakdown."

"Eddie, I am not having a breakdown." I lean my forehead into
my two hands, feeling the burn of tears coming on and not wanting
to give him evidence he can use to have me committed. "I asked for
your support," I say, looking back up at him.

"I *am* being supportive." He lifts his big hands palms up, like a
shrug, a gesture he makes often for emphasis, though other people
use it to express doubt. It's one of the things I once found intriguing

and original that irritates me now. He's a bearlike man, not fat but tall and square, nothing subtle about his face or body. Of course, being gangly as I am, I thought I needed a big man. Or maybe I didn't think at all. Somehow the choices in my life just made themselves, dragging me along behind them. I look the dragged-along part now, that's for sure. I was pretty once. Why didn't I realize that before it was too late and gone? Eddie looks like what he is: a factory supervisor, promoted from the floor, still in his baseball cap, T-shirt, and jeans. Buzzed brown hair graying around the edges, dark-eyed, thick-browed, thick-necked, working on a paunch but not there yet.

Eddie's a man who tries, but his trying only goes as far as he can see, and he needs glasses in the worst way.

"This is *Cal* coming. *Cal.*" I stare at him through the twilight, which is leaching the color from the yard. "Before we got married, you said if you ever met him, you'd beat the shit out of him for what he tried to do. And for getting Nadine hooked, too. *Remember?*"

"Honey, it *was* a long time ago. You said he was drunk and high and you fought him off. Do you think maybe things *might* be different? I mean, it's not like you have to *live* there now or anything. Maybe your parents have a right to see him. He is their son, after all, and it has been . . ."

The look on my face must be what stops him.

"What? What are you saying? How can you take their side on this?" My hands are shaking, and I stick them under my thighs to still them. The evening chill is penetrating my jeans, and now I'm cold all over. "I need to warm up. I'm going in."

"Wait. It's nice out here. I'll grab you a jacket. Want a beer?"

"Yeah, Eddie, you bring me a jacket and a beer." I might as well have said, "Sure, bring me a jacket, a beer, and a very sharp knife." Of course, he misses the danger in my voice.

While he's gone I scan the yard. It's edged with the last spring tulips and hyacinth, red and purple, and I've just stuck marigolds in-between, taking a chance that there won't be another cold snap. In the draining light, the colors look wan, as if they're struggling to survive. We've worked hard to have what we have, more than either of us alone could begin to manage. It was always my dream

to live in a real neighborhood like this, where the houses are fresh
and even as teeth that just got their braces off, rather than ten miles
out of town where I grew up and there was nothing but woods and
pasture. Last year we extended the small patio and bought this padded furniture, or, I should say, my check from the County Eldercare
bought this padded furniture and the gas grill, too.

The longer it takes Eddie to fetch the jacket and the beer, the
more fight seeps out of me. Possibly he knows that. I'm sure he's
faithful, and I should value that above all.

When he comes back, he has my green hooded sweatshirt that
zips, a rare good choice, further defusing me. He puts down my
beer, saying, "I'm sorry. I didn't mean to upset you. I was just thinking of them and how I'd feel. You know, how we feel about our kids.
Like how you are about Carley."

"Goddammit, Eddie, Carley's not the same." The words sound
angry, but my tone just says, *you know this.*

"Carley's done some pretty bad things. She's stolen from you
and from other people. She's a druggie. For all you know, she's
selling—"

My fuse relights. "Fuck you! If you think I need a list of bad
things about my daughter and that's—"

"Jewel, I'm only saying that you still love her."

"Whose side are you on? What is it you want?"

"I'm just sayin'."

"*What* are you saying?"

My husband sits in near darkness perhaps three feet away from
me. I can no longer distinguish his features, and what I pick up
in his voice isn't compassion for my parents, but whining. I listen
to the bugs' and frogs' songs, which are like a low accompaniment
to Eddie's voice as he wheedles on. I have stopped absorbing his
words, though, and focus on the tone. "I just think that you should,"
he's saying, "give it a chance."

And then I get it. "It's the money. It's the $13.85 an hour, isn't it?
You're putting the money I make taking care of them above me.
You damn well can't stand the idea that I said I'll quit if they let Cal
come. You just can't stand to give up the money."

"You're goddamn right we need the money. It's not like taking care of your parents was *my* idea. The whole thing was your plan. Ever heard of a mortgage?" As Eddie's voice rises, Copper rouses and barks.

"What you're worried about isn't the mortgage," I say, and my voice is steel that his flame forged, the law of unintended consequences. He should have known better than to push me. "It's keeping Chastity in tube tops and pedicures and cell phones and writing checks for Rocky's basketball camp and new computer and Nikes and whatever, *whatever.*"

I stand abruptly, intending to go inside, but bump the table and knock over my beer. A little river runs across the table and turns into a waterfall onto Eddie's lap. He pushes his chair back hard saying, "Goddammit." A metal chair leg hooks on a patio rock with enough force as Eddie is trying to stand up that it knocks him behind the knees, and he and the chair go over backward. Flailing, grabbing to catch himself, he clutches the edge of the table, a mistake. It's a sturdy table, but he's a heavy man with more than enough weight to pull it over on top of himself.

I almost leave him there. He'd get the table off himself eventually, I know that, but he fell hard with a visceral *ooh* and a gasp of pain. Streams of Eddie's and my beer spill on us as I squat to lift the table off him. Copper is in a frenzy.

"Are you all right?" I shout to be heard. "*Shh*, Copper. Stop."

"I don't know." Eddie's trying to extricate himself from the chair, but his legs are scrabbling like a bug trying to right itself, and a little mean part of me wants to laugh. Copper is lapping at the beer and Eddie's face, and Eddie is floundering and fending off the dog.

"Can you roll to the side?" I push on one arm of the chair to help. I could more easily lift a sack of cement.

"Oh God, don't do that."

"Should I call an ambulance?"

"No, no, give me a minute. Let me get my breath."

Finally, he does roll the chair and himself to the side. Using all my weight as leverage, I hoist him to his feet, and we make our way into the house with him gimping along, too heavy on my shoulder.

Once we're inside, Eddie eases himself onto the couch. Reclining against a couple of the little red pillows, he mutters, "Shit. Chiropractor's probably closed tomorrow. Would you get me a beer, honey?"

Jaw clamped, I get him a beer from the refrigerator. "Thanks," he says when I hand it to him. Mentally I dare him to ask me for something else.

I go up the half flight of stairs to the bathroom, wash my face, and do what I can to straighten my hair, which mainly involves brushing my ponytail and using spit to finger comb the fringe that circles my face. I root around in a plastic basket of cosmetics I keep in a drawer: honey bronze lipstick, blush, mascara. Smile at myself. A grimace. Try again. Give up.

Back in the family room, I pick up my purse and head for the door to the garage.

"Hey, where you going?" Eddie says.

"To the store."

"Get me some smokes, will you?"

"I'd think if you were so worried about money, you'd cut that out."

Eddie holds his hand up like a stop sign and shakes his head like he's talking to a twelve year old. "Not now, Jewel, don't start up again."

"How dare you! How dare you talk to me like that?"

Eddie's head snaps to attention then. "Whoa. I didn't mean—"

"Eddie, you never *mean*. You just do. Get this through your head. It's their choice. If they have Cal in that house, they won't have me. The agency will just have to send someone else."

Then Eddie swipes at his eyes with the back of his wrist and bare arm. The hair on his arms is fair and sparse, an anomaly on his thick muscles, and the gesture makes him look like a scared child.

"Yeah, Jewel, right," he says.

I lower myself into the red upholstered chair, keeping the coffee table between us. He's still on the couch but has worked himself upright enough to drink his beer. A pillow is stuffed behind the small of his back. "Why are *you* crying, Eddie?" Irritation and puzzlement battle in my mind.

He gives a palms-up shrug, and this time it's a gesture of resignation as he shakes his head. Then he breaks down in the sobs that I've been stifling since the moment Mama said Cal's name. "Rocky said he wants to come live here after he turns twelve next month. Can't do it without this house. Court says boys and girls got to have separate rooms."

"So? Then Lana's got to pay you child support."

"And when's the last time that bitch held a job? The court hasn't even stopped deducting support for Chassie from *my* paycheck, those morons. You tryin' to tell me they'll go after fruitcake Lana and *get* something?"

Eddie gives a deep sniff and wipes his face with the back of one hand. He wants me to feel sorry for him. He wants me to see that he needs a tissue and get him one. I don't.

I tilt my head back to keep any tears from spilling and stare at the line where the ceiling meets the wall for a moment. There's a wallpaper border along the top, a red-and-yellow pattern that I used to like, but now I wish I'd never put it up.

"Who or what would you throw yourself in front of a train for, Eddie?" I say finally.

"What does that have to do with the price of eggs?"

"Not a thing, Eddie. Nothing at all to do with the price of eggs. Just everything to do with weird concepts like, say, love, and"—I palm-slap my forehead—"oh my God, what marriage means."

Sarcasm, no matter how well done, is wasted on Eddie. As I pick up my purse again and head for the door into the garage, he calls from the couch, bleary-voiced.

"You're just going to the store, right?"

"I don't have a suitcase with me if that's what you mean."

"Please, Jewel, honey. Please."

"I'm going to the store."

"Okay. See you in a little while. Don't forget my smokes," he says hopefully.

There's nothing I need at the store. I just need to get away from Eddie, and the Walmart Supercenter out on the far side of town is open all night. The whole area is changing: developers sniffing around, buying up tracts, and putting in neighborhoods where farms used to be. Walmart is cold as a meat locker, and I can't find anything. I'd never go there, but the little IGA has already closed down. It gasped along for six months after Walmart opened but finally choked and held a huge going-out-of-business sale. Bob's Hardware Supply shut down, too, and now Walmart is driving an old local lube place out of business by doing oil changes for $15.95.

I hug my sweatshirt around me, take a cart, and, on impulse, head for the canned goods. Tuna fish, spaghetti sauce with meat, four kinds of soup, carrots, beans, corn, peaches, applesauce, mandarin oranges, then on to dry cereal, spaghetti, boxed macaroni and cheese. Powdered milk. Everything in a can, jar, or box, nothing that needs refrigeration. Where my Carley is living now—still with Roland—electricity comes and goes like weather on the wind, erratic as their bill-paying. Then I swing down a few aisles and pick up some bars of soap, toilet paper and tampons. I'm her mother; I won't let her go hungry, even if it means I have to feed the bum she's with, too. I won't give her money because it will go up her nose, or his.

Eddie gets mad when I buy Carley food or put gas in their wreck on wheels so that she can get to a job interview, which is what she always tells me. He says I should practice *tough love* and cut her off. What he really thinks is that I'm throwing away money that could go to something *worthwhile*, like another skirt that almost covers Chassie's butt. While I'm choosing groceries, I stew on Eddie saying *worthwhile*, and when I check out I don't ask the cashier for a carton of cigarettes for him.

It'll take me forty-five minutes to drive to Carley's and the same amount of time back. I'll listen to old Neil Diamond songs like "I Am, I Said," open the window, and let the night air wash my mind.

"Jesus. Is that your old lady's car?" It was Roland who sounded the alarm, which was one giant amazement to Carley. She hadn't heard a damn thing. Roland claimed that after you've been in jail a couple of times, you develop a sixth sense about when a guard is near, and this wasn't the first time he'd proved that point. Maybe he wasn't nearly as far gone as she was since he'd been out doing a deal until after dark.

He knelt on the bare mattress to peer out the corner of the window. "Yep, it's the Bitch Queen herself, come to save her Princess from the evil frog. Goddamn," he said, grabbing a small plastic bag off the floor and carefully dumping the lines of nose candy laid out on glass back into it. He grabbed up loose straws, a book of matches, a baggie of weed, which he zipped closed, then picked up a pack of rolling papers. All the supplies went into a tan plastic grocery bag that he hurried to stash in the microwave. "Hey, girl! Get up. Get rid of those cans." He was talking about the twelve pack of Budweiser, most of which were crushed cans randomly scattered, much as they were in the cluttered alley in which Jewel's car door was slamming right then. "Does she know what time it is?" He opened a window, then took the two ashtrays and, after looking around, shoved them into the microwave, too. There was just the one room with a kitchen area, and a bathroom. When it came to places to hide things, there weren't a lot of choices.

"Huh?" Carley said, trying to wrap her mind around what he was saying and how fast he was moving when seconds ago they'd been in another time zone and zip code.

Roland got right in her space. He had a narrow face, a thin mustache, and right now his brown eyes were black marbles. There was a waft of beer and weed around him, but it wasn't bad to her. "Never mind. Just move it," he said, and it was loud. He climbed into his own jeans then, not bothering with boxers, which were draped over the lampshade to make the light in the room look cool. Jewel had brought the lampshade once when she'd come with food. Bare lightbulbs upset her for some reason. The boxers were green. "Get in the bathroom," he said, still loud. "Put some water on your face. Brush your teeth. Better yet, get in the shower." He extended his hand and pulled her to her feet, where she teetered on the mattress and then stepped off the four inches onto the floor. "Go!" Roland said. "It's her."

From behind the bathroom door, which Roland had resolutely closed, set to lock as soon as she was inside, Carley listened. Roland had called it right; within seconds she heard banging. The doorbell hadn't ever worked although Roland told the landlord he'd fix it for fifty dollars off the rent three months ago. The noise kept up. If

Roland thought her mother was going to go away, he was forgetting what little he knew of Jewel. He must be stalling. "Carley, *shower!*" she heard him hiss through the bathroom door. She sniffed one of her armpits. Was she that bad? To shut him up she started the water, but there wasn't any hot, which he knew damn well. Another one of Roland's deals with the landlord. Still, Roland was smart, which was one of the things she loved about him; he knew how to take charge in an emergency like this.

"I want to see my daughter." It was her mother's voice, demanding. Not to be fucked with. Roland must have let her in. Carley thought of going out to face her down, but she wasn't too steady on her feet, and Roland's answer stopped her.

"What the hell happened to you?" he said, his voice, mirth mixed in, conveying that it was definitely not good. She imagined him pointing but couldn't figure out at what.

"None of your business. Where is Carley?"

"No, really, did you, like, get into an argument with a blender or something?" Roland guffawed at himself.

"This place is *disgusting*. Carley wasn't raised like this." From the bathroom, Carley heard dishes clattering into the sink. The random sounds of things being gathered up, the rustle of plastic, her mother compulsively cleaning up while she ranted, "And you're on something. It's completely obvious. I can smell the pot, you know. I'm not stupid." Footsteps, heading for the bathroom door. It didn't take very many. "Carley!" Her mother's voice was right outside the door, and Carley startled, jerked her head back from where it was pressed to the fake wood. She'd needed something to lay it against anyway.

"If you're so brilliant at noticing the obvious, then you can hear that she's in the shower," Roland said. He was coming up from behind Jewel, the way it sounded. "Ya'know, I'd a fixed your hair for ya . . . Didn't know you was into punk." Taunting. Carley wondered what he was talking about.

"Get away from me, you . . . criminal. Carley! Come out here, or I'm coming in . . ." Jewel was banging on the bathroom door now, like she had on the front door. She tried the knob, but, of course, it was locked.

"*Criminal* . . . Ohhh, you really know how to hurt a guy. Leave her alone. She'll be out in a few minutes. Or better yet, come another time. Like try calling first."

"Try getting a phone."

"Then you'd call."

She should go out, but it was kind of a weird high listening to Roland bait her mother because he didn't feel the least bit of guilt about it. He told Carley she had nothing to feel guilty about; it was her life, after all. Her life. Her body, her life. She had a right to feel good. Feel great, in fact. She was fine just the way she was.

"Carley!" The bathroom door vibrated against the jamb. Her mother packed a mean punch. She'd slapped Carley once. On the face.

"Hey! Back off, lady. This ain't your house." Roland's voice rose to shout while a thud—her mother's body?—sounded against the door. Carley shrank back, stumbled against the toilet, and fell. The toilet seat clattered down.

"Carley! What's going on?" Another thud against the door. "Take your hands off me." Her mother's words were mixed with Roland yelling something Carley couldn't make out.

"You need to get your fat ass outta here."

"I'll call the police and charge you with assault. Get your hands off me."

"You get the cops here and let's see what they charge your daughter with. Be my guest."

Using the toilet as a crutch, Carley got to her feet, then, as if she were blind, used the sink and the empty towel bars to keep herself upright until she reached the door handle and opened it, using the doorframe to prop herself up.

"Hey, Mom," she said into the fray, trying to sound normal and focus her eyes.

Then, she thought, *Ohmigod. What am I on? Does she really look like that?* and for a moment Carley stood confused into silence. Then she remembered Roland taunting her mother and said, "What the hell happened to your hair?"

Her mother ignored the question. "Carley, I brought you some food and supplies." Jewel was peering at her face, which made Carley want to back up, but there was nowhere to go, and she knew to hold her ground, however shaky. Her mother was the "give her an inch and she takes a football field" type.

Jewel took a step forward, zeroing in for closer scrutiny. "You don't look good, honey. How about I take you someplace. For medical care."

"I don't look good? And you just won the Mrs. America contest . . . Free hairstyling for finalists." That one cracked Roland up. But Carley saw rather than heard him laughing. There was white noise in her head, like a fan or maybe cotton stuffed in her ears, making her own voice echo.

When her mother spoke, she used that tone like she was talking to a moron. It faded in and out, loud then faint. *Wonk, wonk, wonk.* ". . . help . . . medical care . . ."

"Right. Like Nadine got. Locked up with a bunch of loony tunes. Not sick, thanks anyway." Carley thought she might puke on her mother's feet. Standing up was not what she wanted to be doing.

Roland must have seen it. He looked at his watch. "So, Jewel, if there's nothing else you want right now, we were just about to go out."

"Carley . . ." Carley felt her mother's eyes, knew she wanted something. That was the thing; her mother always wanted something.

"We're going out, Mom."

"Where?"

"Just to see some friends."

"I brought you groceries. Can you help me carry them up from the car?"

Roland jumped in. "I'll get 'em." Jewel started to object, but he waved her off and kept going.

Carley's mother took two steps forward and put her arms around Carley. "You know I love you. I want the best for you." If she weakened and lay her head on her mother's shoulder, sank into the soft embrace that would hold her up, her legs would give out, and she'd crumple. Carley locked her knees.

Jewel was stroking her hair when Roland struggled back through the door. He held two bags and shoved two more inside with the side of his foot. Cans spilled out of one. Carley felt a cross between disappointment and relief as her mother hurried over to start picking up the food.

"I'm glad to see you have electricity right now," she said, "but none of this will spoil next week when you don't."

"We're fine," Carley said, afraid to move from where she stood. "I have a job interview on Wednesday."

"Really . . ." Jewel said, and although it wasn't exactly sarcastic, it wasn't a question either, the way she drew it out. It was more like she was saying, *Sure you do.* "Where?"

"Lay off. She doesn't want to jinx it by talking about it, right, baby?" Roland was standing to the side of Carley. She wondered if he realized she was about to keel over. "So, Jewel, we gotta get goin.' Our friends are expecting us and all."

Jewel ignored him. "Honey . . ." Carley didn't look at her mother, but she knew the exact look on her face; she could actually feel it, palpable as cloth, suffocating. "Do you need anything?" Her mother's voice had lost its challenge and was soft and sad.

"Maybe a little cash for gas. So I can get to the interview." Roland always wanted her to try to get cash.

"Give me your keys, and I'll go put gas in it."

"Never mind," Carley said. She had to lie down. She couldn't keep it together long enough for her mother to go and come back.

"You don't have to stay here. He's using you. I'll get you help."

"Hey, she's a grown woman. Why don't you back off? She's just fine the way she is. Ya'wanna see something that needs fixing? Now *that* I can show you . . ." Roland said, loud, pointing at her mother's head.

Nobody said anything else. Her mother turned to leave. As soon as the door shut behind Jewel, Roland hopped from the floor onto the mattress and jumped up and down, laughing. "Ding dong, the witch is dead. Did you see that hair? She's round the bend and beheaded herself to hell. Get it? Headed, beheaded?"

Carley dodged his jumping feet and buckled onto the mattress. She felt like throwing up. So tired of feeling bad every time she saw her mother. So tired of it.

Roland came down on his knees next to her. "Hey, baby, you didn't let her get to you, did you? 'Cause you're perfect."

Bloodlines

"JEWEL SWEARS SHE'LL QUIT coming, you know, the agency will have to get a whole new person to take care of us if we let Cal here," Hack tried softly, Saturday night after they'd listened to the Lawrence Welk rerun on TV.

"She'll be back, she'll be back." Louetta's voice grated like a lawnmower running over rocks.

"What if you're wrong? I don't even know anyone I can hire to do the horses. Chris Hammer's boy moved t' the city."

"Old man, it's time you think about lettin' go of them anyway. Time maybe *I* think about gettin' rid of 'em."

"Tell me something. You hated every person the agency sent. If Jewel quits, you gonna start likin' them? Why we gotta let Cal stay here?"

"You crazy? Seven years since I've seen my son and you're even thinking 'bout tellin' him no?"

"Seven years there was a warrant for his arrest. Statute's run out is all. How you know he's not bringing trouble in his suitcase?"

"The law's not after him now." She was starting to raise her voice. If she were a horse, she'd have broken into a trot and be thinking about cantering.

"Hmmm. You know he wants something. Jewel's good to us. We're trading something good for a problem." He was careful not to wheedle, tried to keep his voice calm and smooth as Moonie's gaits, just make her see the logic of it. If only he could see her face, see how it was playing. To be sure, he'd also like to see if she was winding up to knock him flat. Used to, she'd narrow one eye when she was mad, like she was looking down the barrel of a gun. He imagined she still did. Now he had to listen for danger in her voice and hold very still to sense ominous movement.

"It's her *job*."

"She does more n' that."

"Yeah. The damn horses."

"Not like you were happy with those other ones." He meant the string of home health aides the county agency had sent before Jewel took the job. Louetta had thrown them out like spat-on crumpled napkins the first or second day they were in the house. But this was the trouble with trying to have a conversation with his wife: there was no sticking to the point. She veered him off every time, like a horse refusing to stick to the trail, just taking his head and going off wherever. It wore him out.

God how he missed running his own life. Once he'd been Hack Wheelock and free to love a good horse, good whiskey, and a good lay. Now he couldn't get his hands on any of them. He couldn't see to guide a mount anymore; being ponied behind Jewel was nearly as bad as not riding at all, not that he didn't beg for the chance. Jewel wouldn't bring him whiskey when she brought the groceries; she said he couldn't look out for his wife if he was drunk. He begged to differ, but Jewel was queen of the house now. Just like Louetta was queen of whether or not he got laid, which he didn't; she'd been too moody for years and was too arthritic now anyway. There was no point in asking Jewel to bring him a prostitute since she was so uppity about a little whiskey.

Come to think of it, Jewel was queen of the barn, too. His barn. He'd taught her everything she knew, and now he was unnecessary. Oh, he missed his life, he missed the old days when he'd turned his knack for horses into a living in every sense of the word. His father hadn't had the touch for the mares himself and ended up selling racing and show tack that kept him in the horse world. But Hack—known then by his Baptist christened name, Benjamin Woody, had sponged up the obsession and lexicon as a boy from his father and even more from his grandfather, a breeder who put him on a horse as soon as he had the strength to grip with his thighs. It was apparent early that he had the gift his father lacked. As a teenager he'd ridden some rodeo in Indiana, but his mother's death put an end to that: it wasn't exactly a big money occupation, and his Dad needed him back home unless he could send money. Kentucky was a racing state, not rodeo, and Hack was a hair too tall and big-boned for a jockey, though he could make it as a trainer.

By twenty-one, back living where he'd been raised on his grand-father's failure of a farm east of Danville, he worked in the bourbon distillery by day but saved enough on the side to have bought and raised one chestnut Thoroughbred mare, bred her well, and sad-dle broke and trained her first colt brilliantly before he sold him at a handsome profit. Meanwhile, he had two more up and coming, both fillies, and horse people started to bring him young horses to train. (That first colt he sold had won his first two races out—small stakes to be sure, but it had the sort of out-of-nowhere miracle look that people think is as good as the Rapture.) Hack hired a few hands, redid the barn to state of the art, brought the fences back into repair, and fixed the paddocks. It took a decade, but the place looked like a real horse farm. He was off and galloping.

Along the way he'd married Louetta, mesmerized by the wide, blue-sky roundness of her eyes, the improbability of her perfect gold pageboy, and the way she found him irresistible. For their first date, she tied a short blue scarf around her neck, above a low cut blue top and the cleavage that disappeared into it like hills. He spent most of the evening, watching *Spartacus* at the Bijoux Theatre, trying to simultaneously sneak his arm around her shoulder and hide his erection. He'd considered *The Apartment*, over at the Avon Cinema fifteen minutes away, an obvious date movie, but hadn't been able to resist the horses in the *Spartacus* ad, and Louetta had shone an engaging smile with mostly straight teeth—the front two like Chiclets—while she said either movie was just fine with her.

Louetta had been happy enough to move to the farm. It wasn't that she was a horsewoman, which would have made things a lot easier over the years, but it was as good as any of her other choices, which were none. Not that Hack had realized that at the time; to his eye, she was pretty as mid-spring in the Bluegrass Region and could have crooked her finger to have any man she'd fancied. He was short, bandy-legged, and his cologne was Eau de Horse Pee. He couldn't believe she'd gone out with him, let alone let him feel her up on the second date. They'd married in a hurry, and bang, out came Calvin, a baby who showed up two months before Louetta said he was due, miraculously weighing over eight-and-a-half pounds. That was the first time Hack went blind, before the glaucoma kicked in.

"I can't say what ruined my life, but it wasn't whiskey," he said to Louetta years later, meaning, of course, it was *you*, an egregious insult because she'd had nothing to do with his glaucoma, which was what had stolen both his livelihood and his glory, being with his horses. This was unusual for Hack; he didn't usually bite at Louetta's bait that way. At the time, August heat had gotten to him. That summer had been a killer. Hack worried about whether the hired help was putting enough fly wipe on the horses' faces. It was before Jewel had taken over. No fretting about such things with her in charge, though he'd a thousand times rather been able to do it himself, just for the love of running his hands over their good heads and talking to each in turn while he wiped them down, kept them damn flies from tormenting his beauties.

"That's right. *I* made you go blind. Stubborn old fool too cheap and too stupid to go to a doctor," Louetta had winged back. The oscillating fan blew across him and then away.

"Too broke to go to the doctor since *you* spend half your life there." He knew better. Besides, silence was best because it drove her insane. He'd pulled his handkerchief out of his shirt pocket and wiped the sweat from his face and neck.

"Oh, that's right, I made up being crippled. It's in my mind. I forgot about that."

She'd had a lot to do with everything that went wrong because of her continual yammering. Whiskey might have been involved, too, but he didn't blame himself for that. Having children hadn't helped. They were just bewildering. Their boy sprouted wild hair on his ass before he got any on his chin. Cal was trouble from the word go but all handsome charm to talk his way out. According to Louetta, Jewel was one lie after another without the charm, making up complaints about Cal out of sheer jealousy, and, oh Lord, Hack had to agree that child's looks were something sad: a pudgy giraffe (height from Louetta's father; Cal got it, too) in glasses, hair almost short as a boy's. Louetta gave Jewel chores to teach her responsibility—which worked out just fine for Louetta, Hack noticed. She said Cal was well-liked. And he was; anyone could see he had a following. But the way Louetta took Cal's side on everything? Hack didn't know what that was about.

Louetta said Cal and Jewel looked so different because Jewel took after his side of the family, Cal more after hers. As they grew, it seemed Cal had more knack for people and Jewel for horses, so he supposed she was right. He remembered one time the doctor told Louetta that Jewel seemed depressed, and they should get her some help. Louetta said, "I'll help her all right," and grounded Jewel for lying to the doctor. Cal got arrested three times that year. Under-age drinking, driving without a license, pot and LSD. And after Jewel was gone and Nadine started with the pot in her early teens, well, he guessed maybe she and Cal must be cut from the same cloth. At that point, he didn't know what Nadine looked like to compare their looks, not that he was much given to analyzing his children. Having lost his eyesight, what he thought about was ensuring he didn't lose booze, too. One thing Hack could count on Cal for: a steady supply. All it took was cash. They understood each other that much.

But that was then, this was now. He might be a blind man, but he wasn't blind, so to speak. Cal and Nadine were much as they had been as teenagers, but Jewel was a diamond. What would he do without her? How had his life—well, his and Louetta's both, he guessed—turned out this way? It wasn't something he could stand to think on, the unfairness of things. When Jewel said she'd quit if they let Cal come home, he had a bad feeling she might mean it. Cal was a ne'er-do-well, for sure, and Hack was willing to say no drugs, even no alcohol in the house, now that he'd been dry this long. Maybe that was it: Jewel figured Cal would get Hack himself back on the bottle. But if he tried to say Cal couldn't come, Hack knew damn well that Louetta would start running over his feet with her wheelchair and hiding his cane, to say nothing of the relentless word assault that would make him long to overdose on anything. Except he couldn't. Jewel had taken all the drugs and put them up; she counted them out into little paper cups for them each to take at the right times. His cups were plastic and Louetta's were paper, so he never got confused again and took Louetta's pills by accident, which he'd done once. Just one of his many mistakes, he supposed. He just never knew at the time when he was making one, that was the damn thing.

Both my arms have grocery bags in them, and I'm tilting like a loose saddle, trying to make it to the kitchen counter without spilling anything. Mama and Daddy haven't said a word about Cal since last week when I said my piece as if I mean to act on it, which I do. The tension has been thick as the bean-and-potato soup Mama used to give us too many nights.

"Sorry I'm late." The groceries thud, one bag tips, and celery and toilet paper roll onto the chipped yellow Formica.

"Shoulda made two trips," Mama says. She's in the kitchen playing inspector, as usual.

"You're welcome." With effort, I keep my voice light.

"It's your job."

"Doesn't have to be," I hit back.

"Lou. Quit." Daddy's voice cuts between us, a skinny referee separating heavyweights, from out in the living room. I wouldn't have guessed that he was listening or paying attention. He goes right on before Mama has a chance to ignore him. "Jewel, what's it like outside?"

"Hot, Daddy. Pretty, but hot."

"I'd like to get out to see our beauties. You take me? Get up on Moonbeam, work her out a bit?"

"They're pastured, Daddy, getting plenty of exercise on their own."

"You know it's not the same as being ridden."

"I've got all the laundry to do, and—"

"It's been a long time," he says, and it's the lack of self-pity in the way he says it that makes it pitiful.

"Well, Daddy . . ."

"Don't like to bother you."

I've been half calling from the kitchen, not that it's far, where I'm unloading the groceries, but now I actually walk into the living room where he's sitting in his chair. He's got his boots and jeans on in spite of the heat. Dressed to ride. Seeing that, I get a sick feeling of doom. I try anyway. "It's really not a good day. And it's going to get even hotter, too. Maybe we should wait till it's cooler?"

"Already been waitin'," he says. There's no wheedling in his voice, but it's soft and sad as the petals of the old roses, frowsy and fading now, along the board fence near the road.

When I got up this morning, Eddie started up with me about how we needed the money. I nursed my anger at him while I did the grocery shopping for Mama and Daddy, figuring I'd need it— armor, so to speak. I was right, but it's not enough: I won't be able to turn Daddy down. He won't have to fake what it means to him. He'll touch and call each horse by name without my telling him which is which. When he had his sight, he used to close his eyes as he worked his fingers down each leg, feeling for hot spots. His eyes will be perfectly open and at peace as he does it now. Each horse will lift every hoof in turn when Daddy caresses down a cannon and taps a fetlock, letting Daddy rest it on his thigh and use the hoof pick by feel and memory.

"Moonbeam, my Moonie," he'll croon in the leopard Appaloosa's ear like a lover while he brushes her neck. "How's my sweetheart?" Moonie's coat is white, randomly dotted with many black spots, and her mane and tail stark black. Her nose is that mottled pink, characteristic of the breed, and she *is* a beauty. It kills Daddy that he can't see her striped hooves anymore. The mare will nuzzle Daddy's face, and he'll feed her the sugar cubes that'll be stuffed in his pockets until he starts working on me to tack her up so he can ride.

"Dad, you know I've got to pony you," I'll say.

"No need for a lead, Jewel. We'll be fine." His hand will be linked, easy, relaxed, on her halter, and her head will be still because it's him.

"No way, Daddy. Not safe."

"How about I just give her her head? She knows the way."

He knows perfectly well that any horse can shy and bolt, even a horse as steady and reliable as Moonie: a snake on the trail, a shiny piece of trail trash raised on a breeze, a deer startled from its daybed at just the wrong time, and he could be thrown. He'll argue for what I can't say yes to, so I can't say no to his riding at all. Sometimes I want to kill him for loving horseflesh more than his own flesh and blood. But then there's this: I get it. Sometimes I do, too.

Actually, we could just skip the whole heartbreaking trip to the corral and the ride that will leave him with tears in his blind eyes as

I bring him back to the house afterward. I already feel love leaching my will from me. I won't be able to stay away, deny both of us access to the horses, cut from the same cloth as we are, as he knows. He and I know every detail of their bodies, their lives, as well as I know Carley's. In the end, Eddie will get his way; Mama and Daddy will get their way; Cal will get his way, and I'll get a truckload of anger and sorrow. There's something powerfully wrong with this picture. I should have finished my haircut.

"I've gotta put these groceries away, Daddy, and make your lunch first."

"That's fine. That's good. That way we can stay out the afternoon," he says. Like I couldn't possibly have any plans of my own.

Lean On Me

ONCE I GOT TO wondering if the good a person does counts when it's motivated by guilt, and then I tried to calculate how much of what I do is purely from love. The figuring wore me out.

Then I backed up and tried it this way: who or what would I throw myself in front of a train to save without a blink of hesitation? Carley. So that's love, canyon deep and rock solid. Whatever I do for her counts as love, not guilt, even if I am wearing saddlebags of it at the time. I can't truly say that I feel that way about anyone else. Once I did for Eddie but not anymore. He didn't even understand the question when I asked, stupidly hoping the answer would be, "You, Jewel. I'd throw myself in front of a train for you," and that something essential would come back into focus right then and there for us. And I confess, I wouldn't for my stepchildren. Nor my parents nor my sister. A big heap of guilt there. What I do for them, while there's love mixed in, is born of obligation and never reaches what I call the Train Standard.

It helped me to get that clear, but it hasn't erased how easily I feel guilty about Carley. This morning I sent her over to work at Mama and Daddy's. I think it gives her some dignity to earn what I do for her once in a while. But at the same time, I know that's not why I did it. Since he came, ten days ago, I've avoided Cal as much as I can, going to the farm early in the morning, before he's up, to organize my parents' daily care and keeping my evening visits to the sweet safety of the horses. Today, by having Carley do the Saturday cleaning, I save myself from Cal exposure. Carley and Cal have no relationship; she only knows I don't get along with him. He'll just be a stranger in the house that she has to vacuum and dust around.

I end up with something I crave and don't know how to use: free time.

I make iced tea, take it out to the patio, and try to sit in the lounge chair to start a novel Tina at work loaned me two months ago, but I keep looking up and seeing the weeds, how they are strangling the begonias like too many people in the space of a life, no room to breathe. I have to get up and pull them.

The weeds pulled, I go into the house, put in a load of laundry, and come back out to try to read again. The sun has slid southwest like a yolk on a crooked blue plate, and I move my chair out of the shade cast by the wide arms of the white oak. Restless, I fuss that I'm letting this small miracle slip from me. Eddie's gone to see about moving Rocky in with us and taken Chassie with him; Copper and I have the house to ourselves.

I run a lavender bubble bath and get in with a glass of white wine, and *Music To Relax By* on the CD player in the family room. Eddie, a good ol' boy, says he cannot abide that wussy stuff. He plays country music and AM talk radio.

I catch the guilt that runs over and through me like a wily wildcat with sharp claws, stuff it into a box, and tape it shut. I put it out of the bathroom, lie back, and luxuriate. Even through the closed door, I hear it squalling, fighting to get out. Still, I leave it there for a half hour before I get out and dry myself. Dressed again, I pick up the box and my car keys. The box can go in the trunk of the car for now. I have more time before Carley should be finished with cleaning and laundry at Mama's. I'll go later to help her clean up after their dinner and check to make sure everything is done right. Afterward I'll take her to the Stop N' Shop, load her trunk with groceries, and gas up her car. I worry less when I know she has food. Meanwhile, I'll get away from the house, where I can't stop working, and take Copper for a walk. Eddie says I'm addicted to work and don't know *how* to stop. He says, "Hey siddown, will ya? relax, your mother doesn't live here." It rolls off his tongue like a marble, all one phrase. Of course, Eddie's the one who keeps bringing more kids into the house, too.

The park has trails through woods, and their deep cool makes me long to be on Spice. Copper, a true beagle quite unfazed by his early obedience training, bays at every wildlife scent and hurls himself to the limit of the leash to track it. Reining him in is constant and tiring, and I remind myself that Copper is always like this in the woods. I brought him because he loves it. I know this by the furious back and forth of his tail, the way his twenty-five-foot

extension leash stretches taut, and, yes, I know in advance that
it'll be caught in underbrush again and again, each time requiring
that I untangle him. I do it to make Copper happy. If he's happy,
I'm okay.

I blame Eddie, but I repeat my life with my parents. Everywhere.

There's not a lot of gravel left on the driveway for my tires to bite. It
and the dirt beneath are as indistinguishable from one another as
an old married couple. I pull up next to Carley's dented, rusted-out
heap. When I come in the front door and stick my head into the
living room, Mama looks surprised to see me.

"Thought you weren't comin," she says. "Carley's here."

"I heard her car," Daddy says.

"You hear what nobody else alive hears," Mama retorts. "Coulda
told me. She scared me, showin' up like some kinda ghost."

"I know Carley's here, Mama. I sent her, remember?" Mama
looks hot, some of her wispy hair sticking to her forehead like extra
veins, although the dusky six o'clock shadows are stretched out on
a lovely breeze. She and Daddy both have too much clothing on,
Daddy in his tan-and-green plaid long-sleeved fall shirt, completely
out of season. They were still in their nightclothes when I was here
this morning. Carley should have had them change to lighter shirts.
I cross the living room and start opening windows much wider than
the inch they're cracked. "Good grief, why aren't these open? Carley?" I throw my voice to the bedroom where I assume she must be.

"She's out in the barn." Daddy says.

"What's she doing there?"

"Cal's out in the barn working on the watering system. I sent
Carley out to give him a hand. Hard to fool with the lines and reach
for the tools at the same time. You know."

I breathe in to keep hysteria out of my voice. "Does he have
booze or pot? Or anything?"

Mama says, "We told him no drugs, no liquor. Already told you
that."

"You *know* Carley has a problem. I sent her to work in the *house*
because you'd be right there to see that she didn't use anything." As
I speak, I head toward the back door, the one closest to the barn.

"Wanna get that system fixed 'fore the horses need it," I hear Daddy call after me, on defense. "Cal knows that stuff better n' you. Knew you wouldn't give him a hand."

How long has she been out in the barn with Cal? On my way through the kitchen I see their lunch dishes still on the table. Carley hasn't cleaned the kitchen, which means they haven't been given their dinner yet. I fixed it early this morning; all she had to do was heat it up and make them salad. Did she even do the cleaning and laundry? I'm angry enough to pause and shout before I let the screen door bang behind me. "What were you thinking? You didn't need to send Carley out. What were you thinking?"

But I know what my father was thinking. What he's always thinking: about what he loves and would save above all.

I break into a run crossing the yard, and my first instinct is to scream Carley's name over and over all the way like a tornado siren, but I don't. I want to catch them smoking pot or snorting crack or shooting up whatever poison they're putting in their bodies, because I know that's what's going on. There's no way my brother is actually fixing the watering system with Carley handing him tools. I know him.

The air conditioner in the tack room is running, so I head for that door rather than the main barn doors, which, had he been working, should have been open to let in better light. I approach the tack room door sideways, then duck underneath the window so that I can get to the doorknob without anyone inside seeing me. Not that I think they won't be too wasted to fake being sober; I'm hoping to confiscate what they're using. I don't want either one of them to have a chance to bury it in the barn like Copper sneaking off with the spoils of a forbidden hunt.

As I flatten my body against the barn siding to slide in with as little warning as possible, a cold bolt of fear enters me. It's not enough to neutralize the heat of my anger, though. Nothing could be that cold. I open the door and press through, careful to close it soundlessly behind me.

The old air conditioner turned on high combines its noise with the floor fan, which is angled into the barn. Still in the tack room, I work my way over to the open door into the barn and wait a moment, straining to hear voices over the rattly duet. Nothing.

I tiptoe into the main part of the barn. The toolbox is on the floor, open, broken pieces of straw and crushed beer cans around it. I crouch down, give my eyes time to adjust to the charcoal light. Maybe they've gone? But no, Carley's car is here. The barn is cooler than the house, dark and ominous as a cave.

Then I notice: more random pieces of straw on the floor near Moonbeam's stall. I swing my eyes over to where the leftover bales are stored. One stack is several bales short. I didn't leave it that way, and I cleaned the whole barn floor when I pastured the horses.

In my mind, a complete picture appears. They are in Moonie's stall sitting on bales of straw, shooting up. I turn around and here's my intention, as God be my witness: to get one of the guns out of the tack room from the locked closet and use it to force Cal to turn over his stash. He'll remember the rifle and pistol are kept loaded; on a farm you want to be ready if a snake or coyote is threatening your horses. Cal knows I'm a good shot, he knows I hate him, and, if he hasn't fried his last brain cell, he remembers why. I can shoot to wound. It ought to be enough to scare him.

I hear a grunting sound, like they have some of the animals in there with them. The sweetish smell of pot sorts itself through the summer barn air. Then a laugh and the sound of a slap, flesh on flesh, Cal's voice saying, "Come on, baby," and her laughter. Outrage thuds in my chest. One more step and I'm looking over the stall door.

I'm looking at Cal, naked and scarred, riding my beauty, Carley, who's on her back, just as naked, just as scarred. Legs in the air, her hands are on his rear while he thrusts himself up and into her over and over. Some saddle blankets from the tack room—how could I not have noticed them missing?—are underneath them. They don't even know I'm there until I say, "Carla, get out from under that pile of horseshit," my voice molten with rage. I let them hear me flip the safety off the pistol and I point it dead steady at what no man wants shot off, which is exposed like a bull's-eye when Cal pulls away. "Just had to go for it again, Cal? Wasn't enough to go after your sister?"

Carley rolls on her side, toward me. She looks at my face, she looks at the pistol, and in the slow motion of someone drunk or stoned or high, she looks back at the pistol then at the trajectory. Then she looks at Cal's dick, which is retreating like a scared puppy.

"Not so big and brave as thirty seconds ago, huh, Cal? Doesn't matter how tiny it gets, I can still blow it off." Cal starts to cover himself with one hand, and I say, "Oh no, not one muscle. Don't you move a muscle, Calvin. You get up, Carley. Get your clothes on."

Carley still has only shifted to her hip and floundered between her elbow and her hands as if her body has been dipped in cement and is too heavy for her to lift. My peripheral vision takes in the straw-bale table arrangement behind Cal, the glass tube there, torn-up steel wool, more beer cans, the ridiculous innocence of pretzels.

"Get *out*, Carley. Get out *now*."

She finally manages to get a knee underneath her, two hands and one foot down, then she uses the stall wall for support and makes it to her feet. As she moves, Spice's saddle blanket, a brilliant red, catches my eye and sickens me; I bought it new for him a few months ago, knowing the pure scarlet would be beautiful against the black sheen of his coat. Carley knows it's his. Now though, what's far worse: in the dim light, my daughter's upright naked body gleams a sickly grayish white, her ribs countable, hip bones jutting like fins. The piercings that line her ears are largely hidden by the hair that's fallen free of her ponytail, but everything her clothes have let me miss, I see too clearly. The blackish color at the ends of her fingers is not dried blood, I know that. She hasn't bitten Cal. But the rest of what I see is not mistakable, not even to a mother who delivers weekly casseroles of hope and denial.

"*Carla!*" I have to repeat her name to get her to look away from the pistol up to my face. "Carla. Put your clothes on." It sounds almost gentle as it comes out, but it's actually a hybrid gurgle of fury and heartbreak.

Glued down, she looks at the flurry of clothing tossed on the plank floor as if it were a nest of snakes. Cal's things are mingled with hers. I take a couple of steps sideways, crouch down while keeping my aim true, and fish out Carley's clothes. Hot-pink underpants, black shorts, a black tube top that could pass for a headband. I toss them to her one at a time, and she makes feeble, ineffective attempts to catch them, dropping two out of three. With my eyes and head, I tell her again to put them on, and she begins, clumsily, because she won't look at what she's doing, still fixating on the pistol.

"Je . . ." Cal says, starting my name. He's on his knees.

My chest and head are swollen with suppressed tears. The pressure explodes. It would be cheap to say I don't know what happens next or it happens too fast or any of the things they say in courtroom scenes on TV. In a way it's the truth, but what I really mean is that I stop thinking. "Shut up," I say, and my voice surprises me again, coming out like an animal snap this time, the syllables grating over my teeth. "Shut up, shut up," and as I'm shouting now, I pull the trigger, even though, yes, I see Carley stick out her hand, hear her scream, "Mom, no."

The kick of the pistol stuns me. I can't remember when I've last shot; perhaps it was five or six summers ago when I killed a cottonmouth on a brilliant day at the larger spring-fed pond where the horses drink. It wasn't like this, here, in the darkness of the barn, this amazement of flash and noise and jolt mixing with Carley's scream. Stupid and leaden, I first look at the gun—for what I don't know—then look up to see Carley wobbling at the knees and falling over Cal. There's blood on her, blood on him, and in the eternity before I drop the gun and run forward, I have no idea where the blood began or where it will end.

"What the hell is this?" Eddie demands through the dog's cacophony as I half carry, half drag Carley through the door into the kitchen, supporting her with one arm around her waist, cradling her, as she gingerly holds the hand that's wrapped in a third of a roll of paper toweling from the tack room and two purple towels from Mama and Daddy's house. The towels were blue until Carley's blood seeped through.

"She shot me," Carley sobs, stumbling out of my grasp.

Eddie gapes at me and turns on the kitchen light, a sudden glare. "Shut up, Copper," he shouts, and then, to Carley, "What? What the hell?"

Her face is a smeared red tulip of tears and mascara. She crumples to the floor, supporting her back against the cabinets. Being the mother I wanted for myself, I am pulling clean dish towels from the drawer to take care of her.

"Eddie, listen to me. I need help."

Carley huddles, moaning, crying, protesting, accusing when she has enough breath for words, then lapsing back into pained gasping noise.

"It was an accident," I say.

"Not!"

"Oh my God, Carley, I've said it and said it. I would never, never hurt you. It *was* an accident. Eddie," I look up from where I am crouched over Carley, her wrapped hand in my own while I put more clean towels around it. I don't dare remove the paper towels, though they're soaked. Eddie's face has gone pale in the glare of the overhead light. His eyes are wide with alarm, and when they shift to me, they say, *what kind of monster are you?*

"*Eddie! Please,* for God's sake. Help me. It was an *accident.* I need you to call Summer Milliner."

Eddie wipes his face with a big working hand. He used to bite his nails when he was a kid, but he's stopped that. Still, they are rough and nicked from work, and the right hand he presses on his forehead is cigarette-stained. "Dr. Milliner?" he says.

"Her number is on the list by the phone."

He doesn't move, only turns his head a few degrees to look at me sideways. I'm putting pressure on Carley's wound. "Eddie, just call and ask her to come. She's a friend. Tell her it's an emergency."

"The vet?"

"She's my friend. She can take care of this. It needs cleaning and stitching, that's all."

Eddie's face is a blank. He shakes his head not so much in disagreement but as if to clear it. "Rocky's upstairs," he says.

Carley is crying stridently through Eddie's and my argument. "Now I'm a horse? A fucking horse? Ow, ow . . ." Her face is a grimace as she tries to jerk her hand away from me while I'm fighting to maintain a grip on it so I can keep pressing the wound to stanch the bleeding. She's slurry, and her eyes are not right.

I look at my husband, tears rising in my eyes. *Now,* I tell him silently. Now. Now is the time to help your wife.

"No, Carley, of course not. Summer is your friend, too. You used to help her when she came to the barn. Listen to me. *Listen.*" I wipe her face with a dish towel I've wet with warm water, and this time

she lets me. Two more beats while Carley sniffs and I give up on
Eddie, setting him on a back shelf in my mind for thought later when
I can afford time to be bitter and sad. As we drove here from Mama
and Daddy's, Carley was hysterical, and it was all I could do to concentrate on the road. I'd been afraid to pull over—the gun was, after
all, in my trunk, and the bullet that had lashed Carley's hand, scarcely
scratched Cal's thigh, and been blunted by the mattress of saddle
blankets before hitting the floor of the stall—was in the pocket of my
jeans. Then all I could think of was getting home and getting help.

"Carley, honey, listen to me. Take your hand and keep pressing
on the wound, like this, okay. Press it hard. That stops the bleeding."
I put my hands on either side of her face, but she lowers her head
and I let her, dropping my hands to the tops of her arms and rubbing them lightly. "I'm going to call Summer. *Listen*, honey," I say
when she starts to protest again. "This is a gunshot wound. A regular doctor in or out of the hospital will have no choice. It has to be
reported to the police. They'll question you. They'll question me. I'll
be arrested, but that's not my main concern. You're underage, and
you're a lot more than drunk. You'll be tested, alcohol and drugs.
You hear me? First you'll blow drunk, then the drug screen will
show whatever you're on . . . I'll be tested too, but so what? I'm cold
sober." Carley's head, which she's kept down staring at her wounded
hand and the other pressing the clean towels against it, comes up.
Her eyes, smeared with makeup run amok, meet mine. The whites
have gone bloodshot with her sobs, and their blue looks grayish
black. I put my hands back up to cradle her head, all the silver earrings beneath her loosened hair. "I'll have to tell what happened,
what you were doing, how, where, and why I shot the gun. Can you
see why I don't want the police involved?"

"You *shot* her?" Eddie says incredulously, as if this is the first he's
heard it. "What the hell is going on? Jewel?"

"No, Eddie, there was an accident. Listen, you just go upstairs,
okay? Why don't you get Rocky and take him out to eat or something? Where's Chassie?"

"Out with Frank Ratliff, her new one, the big guy . . ."

I turn back to Carley, who's sobbing louder again. "Okay, honey,
okay," I say and then, eyes still on Carley, "Eddie, just get me the phone,

will you? Then go get Rocky and get out. My car is blocking you, so take it. The keys are in it." I try to keep my voice even, check his feet in their battered Nikes, jeans fretting around the laces. Willing the feet to move.

"If she's high, maybe I better call the cops . . ." he says, moving toward the phone.

"No," Carley shrieks, which tells me all I need to know.

"We told you right along." All the righteous stepfather. His palms go up in the air as he gloms on to one line of a whole story.

"Eddie," I interrupt to divert him. "You don't want Rocky seeing the police here, you know that. And he'd say something to Lana. You get him out the front door, so he won't be involved at all."

"Shit," Eddie mutters and crosses the tile to bring me the phone.

"Now read me the emergency number for Creekside Large Animal Care."

This time he does what I ask.

Summer calmed Carley, cleaned and dressed the wound. She'd brought a local anesthetic and a morphine shot with her. Carley watched her through narrowed, suspicious eyes, but Summer handled her as if she were a skittish yearling, talking, as she does to people and animals, in a voice that's brown sugar–glazed, faintly Southern, quiet, and kind. Her eyes are blue and very direct, but Summer only asked me for ice and a rubber band to keep her pale hair out of her face. Later, she said, "Do you want to tell me what happened?" but it was as my friend, concerned for me, for us.

"I do, I will. I can't thank you enough for coming."

"It's all right. Another time." Then she sat at the breakfast bar and wrote down what we needed to do to take care of Carley's hand. Carley was curled up on the couch, eyes at half-mast, the shot of morphine doing its work.

Now, Summer gone, I cover Carley with an afghan and tuck the edges around her on the couch where the lee of her stomach curves in, leaving space for me between her shoulders and her knees. I stroke her hair, blond roots extending a good three inches now until the November-like fade toward where she dyed it all black. It's leached over time to a dull noncolor, like tree bark against a gray sky on a cold wet day. Her many-studded ear is exposed, and I cannot bear it, suddenly, everything that has invaded my girl's body, and I cry for her, for myself, for all that's lost, and the guilt of what I have done.

I don't know what time it is when Eddie brings Rocky back. They must have gone to a nine o'clock movie after dinner, Eddie making sure he's not around to help in a crisis, I think, and then tell myself to try to be fair, that he did have to get Rocky out of the house. Chassie hasn't come in, I'm pretty sure, since she sounds like an entire cavalry when she does. I've taken the cushions from the living room couch, my pillow, and a blanket to fashion a bed on the floor where Carley would have to step on me were she to try to get up. I don't want her to awaken without my being right there to give her another painkiller. I want to know how she is. I want to put my arms around her when she's awake and try to heal this terrible thing.

It's Eddie who startles me awake, though. "Jewel," he whispers, shaking my shoulder. "Hey, Jewel, I'm back."

"Okay," I say, lifting my head and scanning the room for Rocky or Chassie or both. Relieved, I lie down again and close my eyes briefly.

"Don't go back to sleep. Why's she still here?"

"What?"

"Why's Carla still here?" he says again, furrowing his forehead and looking meaningfully at Carley as if I might have forgotten her name.

"For God's sake, Eddie, where did you think she'd be? I'm taking care of her, just like *we'd* take care of Rocky or Chassie if one of them was hurt."

He misses it. "Yeah, that's what I'm worried about, Rocky and Chassie. We can't have them around this. I mean, what the hell happened? Are the police involved? We've got to get her out of here, that's the first thing. Are you okay, baby?"

"No, no police. I told you, it was an accident, in the barn. Carley was. . . drinking beer with Cal, and I was trying to scare Cal."

"Beer? You said she was high."

"That's what I meant," I lie. I can't tell Eddie what I saw. He won't put his fingers in his ears, but he'd twist it into all Carley's fault, the same way my mother would have made it mine. "Where's Rocky?" I say, knowing I can divert him.

"Up in bed," he says, falling in line. "Is Chassie in?"

"Not that I know of. I fell asleep."

He checks his watch. "I don't know about this Frank guy. He's older. She'd better be up there. I kept Rocky out way too late, took him to the new *Stars Wars* movie. You're taking Carley back to her place in the morning, right?"

I'd hoped not to take this on tonight. Carley snorts in her sleep, which galvanizes me to my knees to check on her as Eddie backs up in alarm, but she's not stirring. Her lips are dry from breathing through her mouth, and I add it to my mental list to put something on them for her.

"Not here," I whisper, sighing and pointing to the formal living room, a place where nothing ever happens except bad news and difficult private conversations. It came with the house, as one always does.

"I'll run up and see if Chassie's in and check on Rocky, make sure he's asleep," he says.

You weren't worried about waking Carley, and the silent words are like the bitter skin of an orange around my heart. "I'll wait for you," I give him aloud. Draping the blanket around me, I head for the living room where I turn on two inadequate lights and survey the formal neutrality, which won't last.

When Eddie comes down, he detours into the kitchen, and I hear the refrigerator open. When he appears, he's carrying two bottles of beer and a bag of popcorn. "Chassie's not home yet. Rocky's asleep. Thought you might be hungry," he says, which means that he is.

"I'll take the beer," I say, thinking I should never drink anything ever again; it could connect me to what happened. I pop the top.

Eddie looks hot and sticky. His white cotton T-shirt, rumpled, shapeless, old, says *UK Basketball* in big blue script. I've told him to throw it out, but it's a favorite of his in that irrational way men have with terrible shirts. "You cold?" he says, disbelief in his voice.

"I got chilly when I was lying down," I say. We are both avoiding the topic at hand. Impatience gets the best of me again, even though I know it would be best to stay low. "I'm keeping Carley here for now. She needs to be taken care of, and Roland won't do it. He wouldn't know how, for one."

"Whoa. I thought we had an agreement about this. Carley doesn't live here."

"Agreements change. I'm changing it." Eddie's eyes widen. Before he has a chance to answer, I throw down the rest. "Not only that, Eddie. I'm quitting at Mama and Daddy's. I won't go back there. I'm taking care of Carley and getting her well, and that's it."

"Whoa. You can't just quit."

"Eddie, quit saying *whoa* to me like you're some sort of cowboy. You couldn't ride a horse on a merry-go-round. I can quit and I have."

"You mean you told them?"

"Not yet. Doesn't matter. I'm not going back."

"Because Carley and Cal drank beer? How's that your parents' fault?"

"Please don't pretend it's my parents you care about. It's my paycheck from the county you've got stuck up your butt, and it's not because Carley and Cal drank beer that I'm quitting. It's because they let Cal come back and stay there, and I told them I'd quit if they did. So now I'm quitting. Nothing I do is enough for them to . . . what? Care? Whatever. I told you I have to change my life." Tumblers are clicking in my mind. "No more everybody's patsy. The county will send someone else. I'll call the office in the morning. They have emergency replacements. It happens all the time."

He's reeling, I can tell. I'd put fire in my eyes and voice, and it suddenly extinguishes, leaving me ashy. I sink against the back of the upholstered chair. Eddie is sitting across from me on the cushionless couch, and he looks ridiculous, his knees too high, his ass too low. "I'm going to sleep," I say into the cavern between us and clamber up, dragging the blanket with me to head back to my spot next to Carley.

Carley wakes once during the night, and I help her to the bathroom as if she were a groggy child again. Two of the Percocet left over from Eddie's dislocated shoulder and she's soon back to sleep. When those are used up, if I have to, I can call my doctor, say I've thrown my back out again, and there'll be a prescription for Vicodin at the pharmacy. I close my eyes against thoughts of Eddie and refuse to let myself check whether Chassie's still out.

In the morning, Carley is asleep when Eddie appears in the dim kitchen. I've made a pot of coffee and used my hands to rinse my face in cool kitchen faucet water. Eddie's in the same clothes he was last night, as am I. "I'm going to kill that Frank," he greets me. "Chassie didn't come home last night. And she's not answering her cell phone."

"It's not exactly the first time," I say and pour him a mug of coffee. "She's probably at Tiffany's and she'll call you when she wakes up with some perfectly fine excuse. You like Tiffany. She's reliable, and Chassie *is* eighteen, not that I think she should stay out without telling you. But please keep your voice down. As long as Carley's asleep, she's not in pain."

He stands, arms crossed on his chest, feet wide, at the edge of the breakfast bar dividing the kitchen from the family room. He ignores the coffee I've set near him. "When are you going to your parents' house?"

I stare at him. "Didn't you hear me last night? I quit. I quit, therefore I'm not going." I say it slowly as if I'm talking to the disabled, which I think I am.

"You mean you're just not showing up?"

"I called the office and left a message on the machine."

"You're not going to tell your parents?"

"They'll figure it out."

"What about the horses?"

I know what he's thinking. This is his ace, which it took him all night to come up with. He's thinking that I'll never be able to stay away from the horses. The truth is, I don't know how I'll bear it. He'd use what I love against me.

I won't let him know how it hurts. "Eddie, they're pastured. They're fine right now." The kitchen and family room are still a hushed gray because they have a southern exposure, but down the hall the entryway is expanding with morning sun, the sidelights of the front door spreading light down the hallway. I gesture in that direction pointlessly, as if the sun doesn't shine in other seasons. "See? Summertime. And don't pretend you care about them, anyway."

"What about your parents' medicine? You can't just not show up."

"I told you, I left a message. Eldercare has a list of substitutes for emergencies. People get sick or quit all the time."

"This is so wrong," he says, shaking his head. "I can't believe you'd do your own parents like this."

"Eddie, as you keep pointing out, it's a paid job. Which means I have every right to quit. My mother quit on me when I was a kid. I'm done trying to make her love me." The sentences spit themselves out of some vehement wind tunnel and drift toward the ground. I think, *Oh, is that true?* But I don't stop and pick the words up and neither does Eddie, so I go on. "If you're so worried, then you go over there."

"Maybe I will," he says, palms up. "I'm going out lookin' for Chassie anyway. Maybe I just will go over there." He runs his hands over his face, a dry wash, and clomps in front of me toward the door into the garage.

The truth is, I don't know what I'll do about the horses. I only know that for right now they're safe in the pasture and that I will put my mind and hands to fixing my daughter, who will wake angry and hungry for something other than breakfast and mother love, mother guilt.

Independence

EDDIE WAS SO WORKED up before he left the house that he forgot to look up Chassie's boyfriend's address, so ended up just driving. He was flummoxed. First Jewel made her own hair look like a crackhead cut it with a chainsaw, then she shot her druggie daughter and brought Carley home to be patched up by a vet, but she blamed her parents and quit the County Eldercare Health Services job even though she knew perfectly well they needed the money to keep their house. And Jewel was the sensible one?

What was that stupid thing his mother used to say? *Don't get yourself all in a kerfuffle, Eddie.* Well, he was now, and his brain so scattered his head couldn't hold it anymore. Oh, he was in a mood to whip somebody's ass, and Frank Ratliff was as good a candidate as any, Chassie out cavorting overnight doing God knows what. Meanwhile, Rocky . . .

"Shit!" Eddie slapped his forehead with the heel of his hand. He'd actually forgotten that Rocky was asleep at their house instead of at Lana's. "Goddammit!" He applied the brake heavily and veered to the side of the road intending a U-turn but even as he slowed, he thought better of it. It wasn't even eight-thirty. If nobody dragged Rocky up, he'd stay in bed until eleven or later on the weekend, already starting that teenage crap at twelve. It drove Jewel nuts; she thought kids should be up and doing some chores if they weren't in school, but she wouldn't want him underfoot today. It was a safe bet she wouldn't get him up.

He straightened the pickup and drove on slowly. He was alone right now on the back road, fenced bluegrass pasture on one side, a pond and the entrance to another new subdivision on the other. It occurred to him that this was The Change coming over Jewel. He'd heard about it from men at work, men who used words like *psycho* and *bitch* in the same sentence to describe it. Some of them said women could take hormones and get normal again. "Like a woman could possibly be normal," his buddy Butch had hooted in the break room.

"Butchie, that's not *supportive*," Eddie minced at the time, pretending to hold out a skirt, mocking Jewel.

But damn it, she *wasn't* acting normal, not one bit. How long did The Change take? She could do a hell of a lot of damage at this rate. The idea of talking to Cal wasn't pretty, but somebody had to make it clear to them all that Jewel really wasn't coming. Eddie had a fear that Cal would show up at his house looking for her. What would Jewel do then? Eddie's kids were in that house, for godsake. The guy was a dickhead, and Jewel had reason to hate him.

He drove on, trying to think through an approach, occasionally rubbing the unshaved stubble on his cheeks, chin, and neck. He picked sleep from the corners of his eyes with a hand that was square and nicked. The day was opening bright and clear, the grass still wet and dew-spangled. Maybe today wouldn't be so humid that he couldn't get a breath in all the way.

He still had no plan when he reached his in-laws' home and he knew that wasn't good. He parked next to Carley's battered car and made his way to the front door, taking note that there was no other car there, which meant that the agency hadn't sent somebody yet. He couldn't figure out whether he should be happy about that or not. He used the corroded brass knocker hesitantly and, when no one answered, repeated it louder. When he raised his arm he noticed that his shirt had a sour odor, and it came to him that it was the same one he'd worn yesterday, which had been Saturday, and slept in, on top of the bed. Jewel hadn't even told him to change.

A tall paunchy man in a white muscle shirt, cutoffs, and bare feet flung the door open while walking back into the house. "Cal?" Eddie said to the retreating back.

"Yeah. You from the agency? Old people're in there." He gestured toward the kitchen, turned into the living room, and sprawled on the couch to fixate on the television.

Eddie hedged from where he stood, half in the room, half in the entryway. He could hear Louetta's and Hack's voices. Cal was channel surfing, and all the voices blurred in a collage of sound. It was hotter inside, too hot already. "I'm . . . Eddie. Uh . . . did the agency call?"

Cal kept his gaze on the TV. "Woke up the house. Threw the old people into a dither, wanted me to go get Jewel. Askin' why, why, why."

"So 'm I," Eddie said, trying to stare him down, which was ineffective since he had only the back of Cal's head at which to aim.

"Your wife's a goddamn fruitcake." Cal said, looking over his shoulder at Eddie, his tone angry. "Ya wanna argue the point, look at that haircut."

Eddie was silent for a moment. He pretty much agreed, but Cal looked like he belonged in an asylum himself, what with that missing tooth and wild unshaven face. Eddie remembered he hadn't shaved either, but at least his hair wasn't long enough to be a girl's, all scraggly down around his neck.

"Cal?" Louetta was calling from the kitchen. "Cal! You up? Come here and get down our pills."

"In a minute," Cal called back.

Eddie went into the kitchen. "Hey, Louetta. What do you need? I'll get it."

"Hey, Eddie." Louetta hardly glanced in his direction, as if his being around or pitching in were white-bread ordinary. She was rattled. "I need the pills outta the middle cabinet there." The kitchen table was covered with half-gallon containers of milk and orange juice, used spoons, open cereal boxes, bowls with the remnants of cold cereal. A banana peel languished next to empty juice glasses.

"Sure. Hey, looks like you're doing pretty well here. Good for you." She was still in her nightclothes, and Eddie kept his eyes averted as much as he could because it was a light summer gown. He didn't know if she needed help to get dressed, but wasn't about to offer. Her breasts looked like cantaloupes. He never should have come.

"Took us forty-five minutes to get this much out, and Hack fell off the stool. Just barely caught himself, grabbed the counter edge." She pointed darkly to a child's red step stool now shoved under one of the kitchen chairs. "Medicine's on the top shelf in that middle cabinet, all the different bottles. *Jewel's* gotta come. I never got my bath yesterday, her father neither."

"Cal wouldn't help you? Uh, with breakfast, I mean?"

"Cal's still in the bed. Where's Jewel? County said they'd be sending someone else, that Jewel couldn't come any more. That's wrong."

She brushed at her face where tears had welled over. "I don't want anyone else."

Eddie didn't take that on, just got down the pills and put them on the table. "Do you know which of these to take when?"

"Jewel knows," Hack said. He'd been sitting quiet as cotton at the kitchen table just taking in the talk, neither speaking nor spoken to. "Puts 'em in different cups for me and Lou and lays 'em out for breakfast, lunch, dinner, and bed." Hack was dressed, his shirt buttoned wrong, but dressed nonetheless in old khaki pants and a long-sleeved green striped shirt.

"You don't know?" Eddie said, panic fraying the edge of his voice. He started picking up the bottles and reading the directions, sorting as he did Louetta's on one side, Hack's on the other. "Where are the cups? How does she do it? Cal!"

Cal had no idea. Finally, between the three sighted people arguing about directions and one blind man who thought he knew the pills by feel, they created grab bags for Louetta and Hack in four cups each. Eddie doubted anything was right because they kept confusing themselves and each other, and there were so many medicines. He wanted to get the hell out before the old people started taking stuff and keeling over.

He followed his brother-in-law back into the living room while Hack and Louetta were swallowing their first rounds of capsules and tablets. "Jewel told me how you got Carley high yesterday. I oughta knock the crap outta you. In fact, I oughta kill you myself and more reason than yesterday. Carley's got a bad problem, and Jewel's been tryin' to get her straight. It's a miracle she didn't put a bullet right between your eyes. Wouldn't have missed, either." Eddie jabbed between his own eyes with his forefinger to illustrate.

Cal gave a short mirthless laugh as he resumed his position on the couch and took a cigarette from the box on the table. He tamped the tobacco down by tapping the filter several times on the table, then lit it, double dragging and exhaling before he spoke. A scar on the thumb web of his smoking hand was a sickly white gash. "Yeah. Some problem, that Carley."

Eddie sat down in Hack's chair and lit one of his own. "Look, I don't give a shit about you, but I feel bad about Hack and Lou. Jewel's seriously not coming. Leastwise not for a while. You're gonna have to take care of them till something gets worked out. Louetta throws the agency people out twenty minutes after they get here." An exaggeration. Some had lasted into the second day.

Cal snorted. "Like hell. *I* dunno what to do with them. Nadine can move in the basement, bring her brats with her. You seen that dump she's in now? About to get thrown out anyway."

Eddie hadn't, but he'd briefly seen where Carley lived with Roland, and it turned his stomach. Nadine's must be something like that, he assumed. "Look, man, you obviously don't know Nadine. Been here, done that. A fuckin' fiasco. Those kids destroyed the house, Nadine fed them what Meals on Wheels brought for the old people and didn't cook or clean, help with clothes, and, worse, didn't get your parents their pills. That's when your father had the heart attack. No blood pressure pills, no pills at all, the house full of commotion, and she was stealing his money. Selling stuff outta the house, too. Stupid stuff like lamps and chairs. Jewel had to give them stuff from the apartment she used to have. Hell, no food in the house. When your mother called nine-one-one, they got inside the house, and next thing you know someone called the welfare people on Nadine, and she lost the kids. Went through rehab the second time. Fat lotta good that did, as you might have noticed." He was pleased to see that Cal looked taken aback, the smirk off his face as he flicked an ash.

"When did he have a heart attack?"

"Four years ago last month."

"Nobody told me."

It was Eddie's turn to snort. "Nobody knew where you were." *You asshole*, he wanted to add.

Cal spoke after going quiet for a minute. "Jewel, she'll show up. She's big talk, no action. She'll show up. The horses."

Eddie shook his head. "Man, I'm tellin' you, I'd a said the same thing a month ago. But she's snapped. I'm *tellin'* you. It's not happenin'."

"Shit," Cal said, running both hands over his low forehead and through his rumpled hair.

"Now you're catching on."

Carley's sitting on the closed toilet seat in the upstairs bathroom, and I'm bent over to change the dressing on her hand when Chassie tries to sneak past me to her room. "He already knows you didn't come home last night," I call into the hallway after her. She answers with a violent door slam. "Charming," I mutter.

"Want me to trash her ass for you?" Carley says, a brief truce. Although I've helped her change into an oversized T-shirt and run a warm washcloth over her face, waterproof makeup still circles her eyes after the small battle with it that I lost when she pulled away. She looks like a girl gang member who could take Chassie with no sweat.

"Yes."

"I'd be happy to, but, oops, somebody shot my punching hand when I was unarmed."

"God, Carley, how long are you going to keep this up?" I'm applying the antibiotic ointment, sickened by the blood seeping from the stitches in Carley's hand, the small tail of black thread at both ends, a railroad track going nowhere. "What do you want me to say? You make it sound like I saw Virgin Carla in the stable instead of Carley fucking her own sorry-ass uncle. Unless . . . did he *force* you?" I ask because I must, because I blame Cal, even knowing the truth: I heard her laughing. We stare at each other, and she lowers her eyes first. Tears start down my face, and I back up, leaving her hand on the sink counter like an exposed object.

When I pick her hand back up to work on it again, she yanks it away, wincing from the pressure the movement creates. "I can take care of it myself," she says, meaning, *Don't touch me.*

"Carley, I didn't mean to hurt you. By what I said. Or your hand. Neither one. I just can't stand to have you accusing me." I'm speaking very softly now, and I put my hand on her shoulder and rub it gently. She pulls back but not convincingly, not enough to break our contact. From where I'm standing it's easy to take a step in so that my body is close enough to gather her to me, her head just below my breast. She holds herself stiffly, not relenting yet not fighting either.

"What the fuck is this dog doing in my bed? He's on my pillow!" Chassie shouts. "Who let him in here?" A yelp from Copper, followed by a thud.

Carley sits up straight. "Don't you touch him," she shouts, rising, the girl gang thing looking altogether possible again. I block her with my body. Frustrated to boiling at the lost moment of possibility, I shout down the hall, "Chassie, don't you ever use that language to me again. Get in your room, shut your door, and stay in there until your father comes home. And I don't care if that's next Tuesday." Then I bend over and call in a high whispery voice, slapping my thigh lightly, "Copper, come, boy, come good boy."

"With pleasure," Chassie shouts, and her door slams a second time, Copper skidding out first, obviously with unnecessary help.

"What's the matter, Mom? Forget your gun? I thought you shot whores. That whore even hurt your dog. Why's she special?" As if on cue, Copper noses his way into the bathroom, panting, and squeezes behind me. He goes to Carley as if for protection, putting his paws up on her lap. What he wants is to be picked up and petted, but the ridiculous, infuriating thing about it is that he's my dog, and she doesn't do a damn thing for him. Carley awkwardly scoops him up with her good hand and arm, my little beagle's hind legs scrabbling for purchase on her thigh. I take a deep breath, exhale, and then take another in. In and out I breathe, silent, furious, ashamed, in and out into this terrible black hole between us, until I can pick up the ointment again.

When Eddie finally shows up, I'm alone in the kitchen with a cup of coffee. It feels like a whole day has passed, though the sun hasn't made it into the kitchen yet. It's going to be hot again. I rub my face and eyes. Eddie comes in through the garage and gives me a questioning look.

"Yeah, she's upstairs. I told her to stay in her room until you got home. She's fine. Flipped out about Copper being on her bed again—I guess you left her door open when you were checking to see if she was home—and swore at me. She threw him off pretty hard. The best defense is a good offense."

"She wouldn't mean to hurt him."

"No, of course, Chassie is perfect. And wherever she spent last night, whatever she did, it was doubtless entirely Frank's fault. Where were you?"

Eddie's face gets red. "What? Did she say she was with Frank?"

"That wasn't my point."

"Jesus," Eddie mutters and lumbers to the cabinet for a mug. He pours some coffee and looks out the window over the sink without drinking any. I can't tell if he's inspecting the birdfeeder that hangs over the patio or if I've just pushed his Chassie button too hard. His T-shirt stinks, and he hasn't shaved.

"So where's the druggie daughter of Annie Oakley?" he says, still studying the landscape, letting his bitter tone tell me it was the Chassie button.

I start to go back at him but stop and close my mouth. Then I start over. "Let's not do this Eddie. Let's just . . . not."

He turns just his upper body. "I don't want her here." He's holding the coffee mug in front of his chest, and his cheeks are like red chrysanthemums, his neck blotchy, too.

"Chassie?"

"Carley! I do not want Carley here. Look, I mean, we've got to think about Rocky."

"Well, Carley is staying." An idea comes to me, and I butter my voice to sell it. "Listen to me, Eddie. I'll put her in rehab. In day treatment. The problem with Nadine's treatment was that she was there twenty-four seven, with hardcore junkies under court order who'd been through it twelve times. She just made a bunch of new contacts. The groups and the classes and the therapy were good."

He snorts, shaking his head, back to staring out the window. "Sure. You gonna pack a little lunchbox and braid her hair, too? Just put her on the school bus? How you gonna make her go?"

"I just am. I have to. I will."

There is a long silence, and I think maybe it's over, at least temporarily. Eddie really cared about Carley once, and maybe I have bought some time. "You need a shower," I say, careful to keep my tone kind. "I can make you and Rocky some breakfast if you want to get him up. Chassie, too, after you talk to her." I don't add that I've already fed Carley. No need to bring her up again now.

This bear of a man faces me finally, leaning his heft against the counter. Even though his neck and cheeks are still flushed, for a few seconds I see how fatigue is carving hollows around his dark eyes, and I am sorry and tender.

"I was at your parents' house," he says.

"What? Why would you go there?"

"*Somebody* had to tell them you weren't coming. Nobody from the county was there. I got your parents' pills for them. Your father already fell off a stool trying to get the pills down. If you're not going to show up, maybe you shouldn't put their pills where only a giraffe can reach them."

Anger freeze-dries the softness I felt for him. "Dammit, Eddie, you knew I called the agency. Why'd you have to go over there?"

"I didn't want your brother showing up here looking for you. Which he said your mother asked him to do, just like I thought. And for your information, nobody had gone out to help them. So it's a damn good thing I did go." And he does his annoying palms up thing, as if to say, *See? Case closed.*

I mimic him with a mirror of his gesture and leave the room, heading upstairs to check on Carley, where I will be unwelcome, leaving him to cope with Chassie, Rocky, and his unfed self. We are divided into two camps now, separate families under one roof, something I never wanted, never foresaw.

Of course, Carley's door is locked, as Chassie's is, I assume. What I need around here are a few more teenagers. Fortunately, Rocky is pushing thirteen, and in case there's a shortage of nasty tempers and insanity, his should ripen any day now. Actually, I *want* Chassie's locked, preferably from the outside, so I'm really not complaining about the fact, only the insolence of it.

Carla is a different matter. "Carley," I say quietly, my lips to the crack of the door as I knock. "I need to come in, honey."

"What for?" On the other side, she's surly, but at least she answered.

"I have to talk to you."

"So talk."

"I also need to give you your antibiotic."

"Put it under the door. I have water in here."

"No, honey, that's not sanitary."

"Put it in an envelope."

"Carley, open the door."

"What do you want?"

"Just open the door, please." There's humiliation in begging to have a door opened by a child in your own house. I feel my temper heating. "Look, Carley, I need to give you your pill and I need to talk to you. Open the door now or I'll get the screwdriver and open it myself."

I hear a drawer close and something else bang, and a moment later Carley unlatches the door but doesn't open it. By the time I enter, she's returned to the bed and sat down. "What?" she says.

The room looks disheveled, as if it's been carelessly searched. Even though Carley didn't grow up here, I always wanted her to feel she had a place, and she picked the lavender paint and the white woodwork in this room that Eddie calls the guest room and I call Carley's room. The white lampshade is tilted, a couple of the bureau drawers are open an inch or two, the blinds askew. Even the prints on the wall are off-kilter. "Looking for something?" I say. "If you need to borrow anything, just ask me. I've probably got one."

"I need my pills," she says. "All of them."

"It's only time for your antibiotic. Well, really, not even that for twenty more minutes."

"I'm going back home, so I'll need all of them. And my painkillers, too."

"Carley, you are home."

"Home to Roland."

I consciously try to keep my voice even and fail miserably. "So that stinking addict can get right into your Percocet? Nice street value on those. Or can you trade up? Or are you wanting to double or triple up because you're in withdrawal? No way. The only thing Roland wants you for is sex and the groceries I bring you. What you want him for is a mystery. He's a loser and he's done nothing but drag you into the gutter with him."

"You can't tell me who to love. It's my life and I'm . . ."

Now my finger juts at her chest. "*Listen* to me, little girl. You are *not* going back there. You . . . are . . . going . . . into . . . *rehab*."

Carley fakes a hollow laugh. "Sure. In some fantasy universe of yours. Why would you think I'd do that? Haven't you heard? Rehab's either court order or voluntary. I don't see any court order, and I don't see one coming." From where she's plunked on the double bed, she leans back against the pillows and looks out the window, trying to appear casual about it.

"He'd best not be out there," I say. "Look, you love him, right?"

She nods, suspicious.

"Good, then. Because in my experience, people will do anything to protect someone they love. You'll go into rehab voluntarily for the day treatment program. You'll live here and not see Roland while you're in it, or I will put a private investigator on him to document every buy and every sale he makes—I mean photograph or videotape every move—and then all of it will be turned over to the police."

Carley's face contorts with disbelief and anger, reddening. "That's blackmail. You can't do that."

"Somehow I doubt I'll be prosecuted."

She's shaking her head. "I'm not going to do it. You'd be having me arrested, too."

"That might save your life. It's sure not my preference. But that's not my choice to make."

"What do you mean, 'not your choice'?" Her voice is dregs-bitter, and now she's crying. "You could choose to treat me like an adult, which I am, and butt out. None of this is your business."

"You may be right about that." I sigh. "But I cannot forget how beautiful you were, Carley. Inside and out. I remember when you were little, shining with the horses, my father whispering to me, *Your Carla Rose has the gift.* Animals just came to you. Horses, dogs, the barn cats. And you were so smart in school, funny, kind. So much promise. So I take a shot—bad choice of words there—at giving it back to you. If I'm wrong, it's on me."

"Oh, it's on you all right. It's all on you."

"Here's your antibiotic," I say, taking two vials from my pocket and putting a pink capsule from the first one next to the bottle of water on the bedside table. "Please take it now. You can have your painkiller, too." I parcel out a Percocet. "I brought up a granola bar, to make sure there's enough in your stomach."

"Really? I think I can handle it," she says, mocking, reminding me that she has an exquisite knowledge of narcotics. Her eyes glitter like a distant forest after rain, a forest in which I cannot see the individual trees.

"I need a phone," she says. "Or is that too much?"

"No phone. The only thing I'm going to enable is your getting to rehab. I'll take you over there for the intake assessment tomorrow morning."

"I'm on drugs, you moron. You know, the ones the *vet* gave me. They won't take you when you're using. Or are you saying I can't have painkillers even though you *shot* me?"

I hadn't thought of this, although she could be making it up. "I realize that, Carley," I lie. "But we can go over and talk. I'll check with Summer about what you'll need for your hand, see what the rehab people say, too."

"Better be careful. They have real doctors around rehab centers y'know, not vets. Real doctors who recognize gunshot wounds. I can tell what happened to me. Wanna bet I won't?"

I meet her eyes and shrug. "Let the chips fall, Carla. You tell your story, I'll tell mine. But this drug business is over, one way or the other."

"She'll be back, Louetta said, not waiting for a commercial during *Wheel of Fortune*. "Jewel thinks she's makin' some kinda point is all. She'll be back." She hadn't even been trying to solve the puzzles or reminding Hack what letters Vanna had already turned over. She'd been studying her angel collection, which covered every available spot in the living room and needed dusting badly, trying to fight off doubt. The disarray of the room didn't suggest that the angels were pitching in much.

"No one to blame but yourself," Hack said to Louetta, his voice filled with *I told you so*, and then he shut down.

Louetta was trying to buck the two of them up, but she was scared that she'd gone too far. The problem was she'd gone so far that she wouldn't even know how to cross back over the line if she decided she wanted to. She wasn't going to throw Cal out. He was her son. It wasn't right for Jewel to make her choose between her children. After a five-minute silence, Hack spoke during a commercial. "And you're not? Makin' a point? Only your point is stupid and gonna kill us both. We gotta have help. You can't keep fightin' with every worker the agency sends. Cal's useless. Even you've gotta admit that."

"Look, sooner or later the agency is gonna tell Jewel that nobody else works out. She'll come around that way. And you know it's true. Nobody takes care of us like Jewel." Louetta wheeled her chair the few feet between them and piled Hack's dirty dishes together, moving them off the end table next to him over to the coffee table where he was less likely to knock them over.

"So call her up and tell her you're sorry. Tell her you'll have Cal move on."

"Jewel can't have her way about everything. It'll work out. She'll settle down." She was quiet for a calculated minute, then said, "*You* could do something. You could give him the money."

"We need that money to live on. Let him get a job."

They'd been having some version of this argument daily during their TV shows, the exhaust of their words adding to the summer heat of the room, as Cal never thought to close the blinds according to where the sun was beating against the side of the house or open certain windows according to the possibility of cross-ventilation. Louetta could manage blinds but not opening or closing windows, especially the ones in the living room, which stuck and were too high for someone in a wheelchair, anyway.

Hack, who rarely raised his voice, finally shouted. "You've always picked Cal over Jewel. You pushed her too far this time. Too far."

Like everyone, Louetta had her secrets, and the one about Cal was a doozy. Truth be told, which it never would be, there was a small chance he was Hack's but a lot more chance he wasn't. The alternative was a terrible idea, regardless of its likelihood: it would make Cal the result of a disastrous evening with a married man, one she'd fallen for like a rock through scotch and water, all chiseled good looks and attentive enticement. Louetta had always been one to believe in love at first sight and thought her guardian angel had led her right to it. Turned out the man didn't see it the same way, even said the notion was a bunch of hooey, yet she'd never forgotten him. But had that made her favor Cal?

"You and Jewel, all you two ever loved was the horses. Did'ja ever think, maybe Cal loved *me*?"

"No horse is dumb enough to chase its tail like that." Hack said. "Never once occurred to you he knew how t' play you? Never occurred t' you, a girl needs her mother?"

"I guess nothing ever occurred to *you*, sittin' up at the bar chuggin' down those beers? Wish I had a nickel for every time I had to go up there to haul you home."

"And had a couple yourself before we left," Hack muttered under his breath. Not quite quietly enough.

"Oh right. You callin' *me* a drunk? You think I never knew you got Cal to bring you booze? *I* didn't go blind y'know."

And Jewel would come around. Though when Jewel came back, Louetta decided she was going to be nicer, tell her "thank you." It was possible Hack had some point in there somewhere. There were things Jewel did for her that no one else knew. Like the times Louetta didn't make it to the bathroom, and she'd wait all day or the rest of the night for Jewel to come help her. It was embarrassing, even with the padded pants Jewel had been buying her.

When Louetta heard a car out on the road, her heart would rise thinking, *See, I was right, she's come back.* Late afternoons, when she knew Jewel was finished at the office, she'd position herself near the window because Jewel just might come by to check on the horses. Louetta had a plan. She was going to call out the open window. "Jewel," she'd say. "Come see me, girl." If Jewel was too stubborn and kept walking toward the barn, Louetta would break down and add, "Please." She might even go on to say, "I miss you." Which was so true that she couldn't rehearse the words in her mind; Louetta wasn't one to cry.

Sometimes Louetta couldn't fight off fear. What if she was wrong and Jewel never came? And there was more: her body was acting up. Sometimes it was hard to breathe. Louetta attributed it to the stifling heat when it got to be like a stone on her chest. If Jewel had been around, she might have told her, but she wasn't talking to these strangers the county kept sending in who didn't know how to cut a sandwich straight. So far she'd mainly managed to make it to the bathroom on time, but it was a constant worry. She was trying not to drink much liquid, and she'd cut out taking her water pills. It was a matter of hanging on. Nadine was lost, but this much would work out, and she would have her other two children. Her guardian angels would come through in the end and bring Jewel back.

The Right Thing

EDDIE PROPPED OPEN THE back door into his in-laws'
kitchen with his knee. "Cal?" he panted. "Wanna come give me a
hand here? Cal!" Both arms hugged overloaded paper grocery bags
like too-heavy toddlers, and his left hand clutched the handle of a
plastic jug of milk, sweating as much as he. The heat in the yard was
enough to make a camel beg for mercy. It hadn't rained in days, not
that there was any want of humidity. The screen door slapped his
heel and caught on it. "Cal!"

"I'm comin', and shut up. Person sleepin' here." Cal's voice came
muffled by walls and doors, but there were no footsteps and no sign
of him. Eddie waited, expecting help to appear. When none came,
he dumped the groceries on the table, one bag spilling.

"Dammit, Cal, I need a hand. There's two more bags in the car,
and I'm dyin' here."

"I said I'm comin'." Agitated now. "This ain't exactly something I
can leave half done."

Eddie was already thoroughly pissed off. Cal had called him at
home and said he'd have to bring groceries. Eddie was in such a
hurry to get off the phone before Jewel heard him talking to Cal that
he'd chopped off Cal's story and just said, *What d' ya need*? It didn't
take a genius to figure Jewel's family was in its usual clusterfuck.

He kicked the screen door open with a disgusted sigh and went
back to the truck. When he returned, awkward with the last two
overfull bags, the kitchen was still empty. "Dammit, Cal!" got no
response and he had to put one down to let himself in. Eddie set
the bags on the counter and started toward the living room but was
diverted when he heard sound from the bathroom. He went down
the hall on cat feet and listened outside the door. Louetta was crying.

Cal's voice came through the hollow door. "It's okay, Ma. Don't
worry about it. You wash your face n' come on out. Here, I'll turn
the cold water on for you. I gotta go help Eddie now before *he* shits
himself."

Louetta said something that Eddie couldn't make out. "Ma, that was a joke. I didn't mean nothing by it," Cal said. "S'okay. No need to cry."

Eddie pulled himself back and had almost made it to the kitchen when Cal opened the bathroom door. "Hey, Hack," he covered, calling toward the living room as if that was where he'd been headed all along.

Cal saw right through him. "In the bedroom. Asleep, like I already said." He narrowed his eyes. "So what's the emergency?"

"The *groceries!* The ones you wanted? Some of that stuff needs to be refrigerated, and it's about ninety-five in this oven you call a house."

"And you couldn't find the refrigerator? Jesus, man, I thought you were a foreman. At what? A sheltered workshop?" Cal wasn't budging from the hallway.

"I don't need this." The groceries could melt themselves into an indoor swimming pool for all Eddie cared. He'd be damned if he was going to put them away.

"Buy your damn wife a decent wig and get her over here. They're her parents."

"I hate to break it to you, buddy, but they're your parents, too. The only person whose parents they're not is me. So fuck you and the horse you rode in on." Then it struck Eddie funny, the bit about the horse, and he chuckled.

"What's so amusing?"

"The horse you rode in on. Y'know. You actually do have a horse here. Bunch of 'em."

Cal fought it but broke. His missing tooth showed when he chuckled, obvious as a wheel missing a spoke. The tension between the two men seemed to dissipate or just couldn't keep its shape in the heat.

"Weather sucks, don't it?" Cal said, leaning against the wall. "Hot. Last night I slept in the tack room. Air conditioning," he added when Eddie looked quizzical.

"Oh, yeah. Speaking of horses, they okay?" Eddie guessed it wouldn't be altogether bad if there were some problem with them, one to scare Jewel enough to come.

"Couldn't tell by me. Right number is in the pasture, so none's dead." No longer playing offense, Cal went on by Eddie into the kitchen. Eddie followed him, thinking Cal was going to put the groceries away. Instead, Cal grabbed the crust of a sandwich off a dirty plate and stuffed it in his mouth, then wiped his face with his hand as if something were finished.

"Where's the agency person?" Eddie said.

"She's thrown out two 'emergency substitutes.'" Cal etched quotation marks in the air with his forefingers. "Stubborn old woman. First one could cook, too. I mean *cook*. Ma picks a fight, bitches 'em right out the door."

"Told ya." Palms-up shrug.

"Yeah. You told me." He shook his head. "Crazy old bat. You wondering why there's no food? For one, I got no keys to Carla's piece of crap in the driveway, which makes it tough to use. Anyway, Ma *insisted* the agency girl that came yesterday take her to the store with her when *she* was going to get groceries. Right there, I knew was the end. Tried to warn the chick, but she's goin', 'Oh me, I'll be *fine*. See, I'm, like, *trained* to deal with the elderly and disabled.'" Cal said the last in a high mincing tone, flipping his wrists forward. "She was cute, y'know, and I liked t' watch her bend over to pick up Dad's cane, but, hell, then I just shook my head and told her t' have at it. Knew what was gonna happen."

"Why? You ever done it?" Antagonism, but Cal didn't seem to pick it up.

"Did Jewel ever take Ma to the store with her?" Cal said.

"Nah, she bought groceries on the way here."

"That's cause Jewel actually knows what she's doin'. 'Cept when it comes to hairstyles. What's *that* about?" Eddie knew he should keep it to himself how much he agreed about Jewel's hair, but it was too hard. The men shook their heads, back in concert, and Cal went on. "Soon as you put Ma in the car, which takes the first hour, all you're doin' is rearranging deck chairs on the *Titanic*."

"Huh?"

Cal backed up to lean against a counter and laughed. "Shit, man, they never made it out the driveway in that poor chick's little agency car. A Toyota Tercel, little Tinkertoy, man. Now you know the size of Ma, her with her wheelchair to get out the door, down two steps, across the gravel. Wouldn't fit in the trunk or backseat, of course, but Ma still wants to go, says she'll sit in the car with the air on, or maybe they'll have one of those motorized shopping carts she can ride. So, like forty minutes later, there's Ma finally shoveled into the front seat with her knees wrapped around her ears all the while it's a hundred six in the shade, both of 'em sweatin' like pigs, and then the agency chick loses it when Ma says oops, she has to go to the bathroom. The chick drops the f-bomb, which Ma's virgin ears only heard a million times before, but Ma flips out and bombs her right back along with a few hundred other choice names. It takes another fifteen minutes for her to untangle Ma and get her out of the car, both of 'em sweatin' and swearin' so bad the fire ants dove for cover, and the agency chick zooms off, leaving Ma in her wheelchair in a cloud of Toyota dust."

"She quit?"

"Or Ma threw her out. Or they spent the time fightin' about who could do it first. Dunno. Didn't wanna know. I stayed in the house till the chick was gone. Then I got Ma back in."

"Jesus." As if Cal had handed Eddie a little snapshot out of his wallet, they looked at it together and then at each other, both shaking their heads while the image animated in their minds. The men had a moment of silent communion and then erupted into laughter.

"Shit creek . . ." Cal managed to get out.

"Paddle on the bottom about a half mile back," Eddie choking on mirth, in accord.

Cal used his grungy undershirt, the muscle type, to wipe the sweat off his face, and as he did, the scar on the web of his hand moved across his forehead. Jewel's teeth, defending herself in a different lifetime. Eddie thought Jewel would shoot *him*, shoot to kill if she saw him standing here all easy, laughing with Cal. He swallowed his trail of chuckles like too much spit several times, guilty, confused by his lapse into camaraderie. He took a step backward, which put him against the refrigerator. His head went down into both hands as he tried to clear his mind. Too much at stake, too much. Sometimes you just had to reach down into the muck and pull out what you had to save, he thought. *Do the right thing, Eddie, and things will work out in the end,* his mother used to say. Back when she was alive, she used to annoy the crap out of him with her advice. Now, sometimes it took his breath away how much he missed her, now that he had no one to ask, *What's the right thing?*

"Hey, man, want a beer?" Cal said. "Just keep it on the QT."

"No. Yeah."

Cal laughed. He went into the hallway and toward his parents' bedroom. "Ma, you need anything?" he called in that direction.

A moment later he was back. "Sweet. Both asleep." He opened the refrigerator and rummaged in the far back on the bottom shelf. "Got it pretty well hidden here. Old buddy of mine brings stuff now and then, but I run low. Appreciate it if you could bring more pretty soon or the keys to that heap out there. You got 'em?"

Eddie popped the beer Cal handed him and ignored the question. If he got the keys from Jewel it would be perfectly obvious that he'd been out here, and his ass would be grass for Jewel to mow. "Look, man," he said, unconsciously falling a bit into Cal's lingo and rhythm, "you need cash?" He was trying to figure what it would take to get Cal gone so Jewel might take over again.

"You think I'm here now 'cause I won the lottery? Dragged in on my ass and elbows, man. Figured the folks for some dough, but the old man's"—Cal held up a clenched fist—"tightwad would be generous compared to him." He took a deep slug from the can he held, his head tipped back, eyes closed.

"So what're ya gonna do?" Eddie said after Cal finished swallowing.

"Dunno."

"How much you need?"

Cal shrugged. "Y'know. Living money, beer money, travel money. A stake to get started again." He briefly looked at Eddie with a small question on his face.

"Got nothin' like that much, man. My kids . . ." Eddie said, a slight shake to his head. "Rocky—he's my son—livin' with us now, too. Already had my girl there."

Cal shrugged and pulled a bag of pretzels from the top of the nearest bag of groceries. His hair was greasy, in separate hanks against his neck from the heat, and his skin shone with sweat and oil. In the light from the kitchen door, Eddie could see where Cal and Jewel resembled each other—Jewel would doubtless slap him upside the head were he to say it to her—and it was an echo of Louetta's family height, the heft of her bones more than weight. Jewel had her mother's round blue eyes, too, but Cal's were more like the indeterminate color of dusk. Eddie didn't see Hack in Cal, though he did in his Jewel, in the pronounced high forehead and cheekbones that made her whole face look horsey. These thoughts wove through his head, braiding with another: he was conspiring with the enemy. He figured, hey, you've got to do what you've got to do to take care of your kids. That's always the right thing. He was sure that's what his mother would say. His concern was whether he could get away with it.

"Jewel took the classes, tests, all that crap, got the certification and home care license. She could've worked more hours here at the house, y'know, agency's authorized fifteen more, so she could bill more hours, but no way, not with her regular job," Eddie said.

"So, shit. And your point? She's here zero hours now. Place is fallin' apart and me about to blow my own brains out. Won't have to call Jewel t' do it for me. Folks'll end up in a nursing home in another week when some agency inspector shows up and goes to court about it, and there goes every last cent with 'em."

Eddie had no idea if Cal knew what he was talking about, but he couldn't immediately discount what his brother-in-law was saying, which made his head hurt. His first thought had been to get Cal to move on; he figured that once Cal was gone, Jewel would soften up, and the agency would give her the job back, thrilled not to be teeing up new workers for Louetta to drive out. Once Louetta and Hack were in a nursing home, though, he doubted they'd ever come back out. It just didn't work that way, sure never had in his family. He felt a load of guilt about that, even if it was probably where Louetta and Hack belonged. Seeing what Jewel did for her parents made him question what he'd done for his. They'd died before he knew Jewel. She kept hers in their own house, not that they ever said anything but *kiss my ass* and *we're out of toilet paper* in gratitude. It occurred to him for a moment to wonder who would take care of him if he was crippled, blind, old, if not Jewel. Chassie? She wasn't looking like a great candidate.

Eddie paced back and forth uneasily. "Why don't you put this stuff away?" he said impatiently. "A bunch of it needs to be in the fridge." Jewel would make sure he had a slow, pain-wracked death, he thought. Then she'd divorce him and take the house. On the other hand, he didn't see any other options, and he had his kids to think about.

"Listen, man. Jewel and me, we count on her money from the agency for the house payment. Got my daughter with us, and now my son movin' in, too."

"So you said."

"Can't do without the money."

"She's your wife."

"Can't make her do it. Already tried to get her to. You need cash. I gotta have the income. What if you call the agency, tell 'em you're Hack, tell 'em Jewel's back on the job. She's got the certification, all that crap, like I told you. They don't send inspectors after *her*. You take care of stuff here. I'll help, I'll bring you food. When they got appointments or whatever, I'll take 'em. When Jewel comes to her senses, then she and I won't have lost the house, she won't have lost the job, Hack and Louetta won't be in the nursing home, you'll have enough money to leave, whatever. We'll split the check."

Cal rolled his eyes. "Carley was right."

"What?"

"You are a moron."

Eddie bristled at Cal, even as he filed away what Carley had called him. "Fine. What's *your* plan?" His armpits were wet, his face sticky, and he was aggravated because Cal stood there drinking beer, eating pretzels, and making no move to unload the groceries. The bottom of one of the bags was wet now, the edge of something poking a hole in it. Eddie started pulling packaged food out: bread, macaroni and cheese for the microwave, peanut butter, seedless strawberry jelly, salami, iceberg lettuce, baby carrots, potato chips, chicken pot pies, apples, bananas, Popsicles. "I don't know where this stuff goes, man."

"And I do? I don't have a plan. I'm just not dumb enough to think we could pull this off. Jewel may be a cow, but she's not stupid. What about the agency? I mean, she's gotta turn in records n' stuff like that. You're gonna end up busted for fraud, man. Been there, done that when I was like twenty-three, and I had a hell of a better con going, too."

Eddie guessed he was supposed to punch Cal in the mouth for calling Jewel a cow. He spoke slowly, devising. "We only have to pull it off until you have enough money to move on. She'll likely come back then. Or until she cools down and gets worried enough about the horses and the old people. Either way, it's gonna happen. Could be a while, though. I dunno. Never saw her like this before. I'll go through her stuff at home." He was gathering momentum, convincing himself to convince Cal. "Yeah, she's got forms to fill out, just check marks. Easy stuff, I can do it. And I'm the one who turns in her forms and time sheet anyway, 'cause I pick up her check at the county office. They got her signature on file so I can, 'cause I get outta work before the bank closes. Agency office people see me all the time. They're used to me, nothin' new about that." He paused and put his palms up flat in the air. "It's all we got."

Cal mused for several minutes while Eddie kept silent. At different times, they finished their beers, and when Cal emptied his, he got out two more. Without asking he handed Eddie one, and without comment Eddie took it.

"I ain't doin' this by myself," Cal said, breaking the silence. He started emptying the bags that rested on the kitchen table and righting the groceries that had spilled from the torn bag. "Come on, man. I don't know where this shit goes, either. And I'm goin' on record that I do believe you're gonna go down. Count on me to say I had no idea what you was pullin'. I was just here tryin' to help out, like a good son."

"Just don't call my house. Ever. I've got a cell phone." Eddie tore off a piece of brown bag and rooted through the unwashed dishes and groceries on the counters for something to write with.

Carley stuck out her lower lip to blow her hair back, more to indicate disgust than to cool her face. Another goddamn therapy group.

Harder to completely tune out than the Drug and Alcohol Awareness group, in which patients were expected to just listen. This had
to be the biggest waste of time since high school and the people
sitting in this stupid circle the biggest losers. *How do you feel, Carla?*
What's your responsibility in this, Carla? I think you're making res-
ervations right now, Carla. You're planning where and how you can
get high. Listen up, Carla: Roland is your process, you realize, just
as much as what he supplies, Carla. What better plan can you make
for your life, Carla? You can do something different now, Carla. How
do you feel about what Heather observed about your possible delu-
sions, Carla? One more of their pick-pick-pick questions and she'd
blow. She couldn't breathe without someone up her ass about it. Her
social worker accused her of not investing in her recovery. If that
chick only knew.

"You with us, Carla? I mean here, in the room? What do you
want to say on that subject? Have you started your letter?" Matilda
said. Matilda wasn't her name, which Carley regularly let herself
forget. The aide was fat and very black with enormous boobs and
just looked like someone who should be named Matilda. Carley
used group time to picture Matilda naked on top of some short
white guy, a lawyer probably, the guy having made a serious strategic sexual positioning error and now being crushed to death.

"Uh, nothing right now," Carley said. Too late.

"What was the subject, Carla?"

"I'm, uh, sorry. I'm not sure. My tooth is really hurting. I have a
dentist appointment this afternoon."

"You went to the dentist a couple of days ago."

"It's abscessed. He's doing a . . . root canal, then I get a crown
thing. It'll take like three or four appointments."

"You didn't bring us a note about antibiotics."

"I'm not here court-ordered. I take them at home."

"Don't play me, Carla. Do you want recovery, or don't you?" They
weren't supposed to confront individuals in group, but Matilda
exempted herself from that rule, and Annie Brooks, the blond
social worker who professionally outranked her, let her get away
with it, possibly because her whole head would have fit into one of
Matilda's bra cups.

Carley almost put her head down but saved herself by keeping it up. "Yes."

Matilda kept at her like a woodpecker. "Then follow the rules. Don't give up. Be here. Be at meetings. Don't keep those reservations you're making."

"I'm not. I just have to go to the dentist. I'll be back for the last group." She'd need to make sure she wasn't late for that, or she'd face another round of interrogation and exhortation.

Matilda gave her a hard narrow-eyed stare, but Carley met it.

Pamela Goodie-Goodie, who must have been in treatment for seventeen years, stuck her two cents in from across the circle. "Could the dentist take you after four-thirty?" Carley wanted to do bodily damage to her, sticklike, scarred-up, and as earnest as a poster announcing, *I'm here to help with your recovery 'cause if we don't help each other, none of us will get well.* A few people nodded in agreement, but the ones Carley appreciated were in a different zip code, sprawled with their butts ready to slide off the edges of their chairs and feet emerging like tree roots from under the tables that formed a large, conference-like oblong in the room. Unlike Pamela Goodie-Goodie, they had baseball caps pulled low over their eyes. It made a certain sense; the lights were interrogation-room brightness. A white dry-erase board in the front was smeared with red marker notes from an earlier Alcohol Awareness class, and until now Carley had been entertaining herself by rearranging what words were still legible into dirty sentences.

"No, *Pamela*, the dentist closes early. He's like, *old*." Carley wanted to puke.

"Let's remember to stick to I statements," Annie the social worker said, and for a fleeting moment, Carley liked her. Her eyes were green, and she had long legs and fingers. No piercings, not even her ears, and her clothes were pretty colors that made Carley sad for herself. "Carla, I hope your tooth feels better soon," she added. "I want to emphasize part of what Donna just said. Remember what you've learned about how long withdrawal takes and be strong. If you've made a reservation, don't keep it. Come to group and be honest. All right, let's move on. Does anyone have a letter ready that they're willing to read to the group?"

The letters were what they were supposed to write to their process, the treatment buzzword for whatever addicts use that's become the best friend/lover, whatever is destroying their family, their credit, their health, their sanity and landing them in jail to boot. They kept talking about how sometimes the process is wet like alcohol, and sometimes it's dry like crack. For some people it's both, and for some it includes a person. ("Like Roland," Matilda shot at Carley. "Take your blinders off." Annie finally shot Matilda a look that said *shut up*.) No matter, in every class and every stinking group, they all kept saying *You have to say good-bye and you have to grieve.* That's what the letters were for.

What a crock.

I have to see my horses. I'd already put in for a half day of vacation time today. Mama and Daddy have eye doctor appointments; I know because I made the appointments myself, well before Cal came back to open old graves and new ones. The agency worker will have to take them, and I'm betting that Cal will take the chance to ride into town to buy booze and score whatever else he can. I didn't tell Helen in personnel to cancel my time off, though. At lunchtime, I'll use the bathroom here to change into jeans and boots and drive out past Mama and Daddy's house. If it looks as empty as it should at two o'clock, I'll park a quarter mile down the road, walk the fence line, and go through the back pasture gate. No one's been standing behind the fence banging on a grain bucket to call them in, loving them by hand with carrots and apples and lumps of sugar hidden in a pocket, no one brushing them down, using a hoof pick, checking eyes and ears, applying fly repellent. No one's been working them out, crooning *Good boy, good girl, good, good, so good.* Surely they miss me.

I never thought it would come to this. I thought it would hurt Daddy so much not to have me take him out to his beauties he would make Cal leave. I thought Mama would never put up with agency people. Now, instead, I have lost what I love and I'm going to have to deal with winter, when the horses can't fend for themselves, contently pastured. September is scorching in Kentucky, and it can fool you into thinking summer lasts, but I remember.

Everything I really want is in the barn, but an old bridle that was in the trunk of my car is looped over my shoulder, and I've got a plastic grocery bag with eight carrots and four apples. Sugar cubes in my pockets. I bought a new halter and lead rope, curry brush and hoof pick at the tack store, and they're in a second bag with a new bottle of fly repellent that's supposed to last fourteen days, though I know that's unlikely. I wish I could put fly masks on them now, but it would be a dead giveaway that I was here.

The sun is a bare lightbulb in the sky. I'm shocked at how dry the pasture is, tousled and weedy, though I drive by miles of pasture every day. It's different when your boots are on it and you feel the brown grass crack underfoot, too much dust in the air. The ponds must be low, though I know the horses have enough water. There! My heart runs high when I spot them, desultory in the heat, along the far line where the fence holds back the woods. They're in a ragged circle in the shade, tails at work: Moonbeam swishing flies off Red's face, Spice relying on Red's tail and protecting Moonie's face and withers. Charyzma is just approaching them, returning from the bigger pond where there's also a three-sided run-in shelter; sometimes she likes that shade, but the others rarely use it for that. They like the trees better, it seems. Still, when it storms, it's always comforted me to know they've got it.

I bang the shanks of my wedding rings on the hard plastic bottle of fly repellent, but I'm too far away, and it doesn't carry but Spice's head alerts, and his ears flick forward. The sun is searing the back of my neck and the tops of my shoulders, making my underarms sticky as liniment and putting sweat between my breasts. The bags rustle against my thigh. I think I will die in these jeans and boots, but I wanted to ride so badly that I wore them against all reason. It's too hot to give any of them a good workout; I can't wipe them down properly afterward. If I left them sweaty it would dry in a hard white crusty mess.

On the horizon, roadside trees and the top two-thirds of the barn impose themselves next to the roofline of my parents' house. My mind's eye has Carley's car still in the drive where we left it in that terrible dusk. Even if people were in the house, I think they'd need binoculars to see me from this distance, and I'm keeping to the natural declivities, not that they're great or deep. I rarely spot the horses in the back pasture from the kitchen steps. There are small rises in the land, and the larger pond, the one they gravitate to, is in a low-lying area. I'm afraid to shout to the horses, which is ridiculous, but I trudge on to get within certain earshot.

All the horses' heads are up now, ears inclined toward me. "Spice, Moonie, come on! Get up here, Red! Get your apples. Charyzma! Come on, you beauties!" I hold up an apple and break into tears.

Spice knows it's me. He breaks away from the circle and jogs. Charyzma is crowding him for the lead, and usually he yields but not today. Red's coming from the other side, too. Moonie considers from where she is, then catches right up.

I'm crying, my arms around Spice's neck, kissing him. "My sweet boy, I'm sorry, I'm sorry. I love you." I try to caress each one as they crowd me for the apples and carrots. Now Spice is at my back pocket, nosing for sugar. Flies circle all their faces, and I swipe at them ineffectually.

Like the Pied Piper, I lead them back across the field to the shady fence line by the woods, talking to them steadily: "How have you been? I've missed you so much! Did you know that? Did you miss me, too?" as if we're carrying on a conversation and I'll get a sentient answer. Spice pauses to urinate, and I stop the procession to wait for him. I can put the halter on one at a time, clean hooves, check for sores, brush, and wipe them down with repellent. I can talk and sing and love. Each will keep his or her ears toward me, listening. Each will stand through every attention I give and will not turn away. I'll slip the bridle on each and use the fence for a leg up. Fifteen minutes for each of a light bareback workout: walk, trot, canter, figure eights with some flying lead changes. Each must be cooled down in a walk and then brushed again to make sure I'm not leaving any sweat. Then I'll have to go. It won't be enough. Not for them and not for me.

While I'm up on Spice's back, I try to stay disciplined but keep glancing across the pastures toward the house as I lead him around to check how he's walking. I end up flopped forward with my head on his mane and my arms in a hug around his neck. If emotion were a chemical that dissolved bones, that would explain it. Family. I don't know that I've ever thought about what I feel for them before now in this absence. It doesn't matter whether it's named habit or duty, need or longing, a bravery that makes people avert their eyes from its sadness or the unlikeliness of love. It just doesn't matter. It's inescapable. My parents drove me away, and I left. Yet every day the phone rings and it's not my mother, not my father, I'm hurt again. And I think this: really, I'm doing this to hurt them back. It's got to be killing Daddy not to be able to be with the horses, just like it's killing me. Good. Mama's got to be going crazy with the agency people. Well, fine. I've always given in. Not this time.

I try the crook of my arm to clear my own sweat, which runs down my face and confuses itself into the stale tears that have been starting and stopping the whole time I've been here. There's too much, and I end up having to take off my shirt, wipe myself down, and put it back on when I groom Charyzma last, remembering when her foal Dance was born.

It was Carley who put together the foaling kit. And Carley put down every bit of the straw for the foaling stall. It was ready a good four weeks before Charyzma was due. She used a warm washcloth on Charyzma's teats as soon as she started to bag up because Daddy told her it would help a mare get ready to nurse. We both cried when Dance came out, and, oh my God, when he first got up on his feet! "Remember how beautiful that was, girl? Dance all wobbly and trying to nurse and Carley helping him find your teat, with Daddy telling her what to do. You were always such a good mother. I thought I was one, too. We nursed our babies, didn't we girl? We took care of them." I stroke her forehead and then lay my face against hers. "I don't know what happened, Charyzma. I tried, I really tried. She used to be so different than she is now, and I've just lost the knack. She's gone. Everything's gone. I don't know when I'll be back." I say it again, crying, to each of them. "I'm so sorry. Be good. Be careful. I love you. I don't know when I'll be back."

I've allowed forty minutes to make it to the rehab center before the day treatment staff leaves. I drive with windows open and air conditioning on high, adding to the worry folder in the drawer of my mind labeled *Horses*, next to the one for *Winter*, when the horses will need better shelter, hay, and grain. Charyzma, especially, will need to be reshod soon. We need the farrier out there. He's scheduled to come the last of the month. But I can't think about that now, so I try opening the *Carley* drawer of my mind instead.

I know Crossroads Center from when Nadine was an inpatient. They're good about letting family know what's going on. Without "breaking confidentiality," as they put it, they let you know if things are "going well" or "not so much." Depending on who's around and who's not, it's possible to pick up little beads of information from different staff, like pearls scattered from a broken necklace, and string them together on your own. The trick is to be there. Nobody will say anything over the phone. Any nurse or aide could get nailed for breaking the law, but almost every one of them has a heart. They have their own histories. Half the nurses have professional manicures or frosted hair or both, but, still, they have their own lives to endure, and on some faces the texture of the past or present shows. The male staff have an earring in one ear, bleach their hair like the women, and it seems everyone sports a cross hanging from a necklace, the more ornate the better, as if it's part of the unisex uniform: navy or maroon scrubs over a T-shirt, white shoes, Crossroads ID badge, crucifix.

It's a brick-and-concrete building, new enough and really not the dead ringer for a prison that Carley makes it out to be. As if she'd know. Gardens at either side of the entrance in front of the shrubbery look like they have a case of heat exhaustion: some gone-to-seed red-and-white geraniums and silver-white dusty miller that's already bolted, wilted and flopped over, arranged in-between. *Oh hell, who cares?* is the message from the maintenance department. Half-mature silver maples measure the parking lot, with benches between where day treatment patients who don't have licenses or cars anymore wait for their rides. And after they hit the vending machines, practically everyone congregates out there to smoke between classes and therapy sessions. This probably used to be a farm, which is why the land was already cleared. Some family had to sell their home. A family like mine.

A bus stop is tucked by the highway frontage, a little weather shelter with a bench inside. Since she's not here by court order, Carley can sign herself in each day, but I've insisted on driving her back and forth. It comforts me to wait in the car and watch her walk in the door in the morning and walk back out in the afternoon. It's starting to cause a problem at work, though I'm working through my lunch hour to make up for leaving to pick her up and then going back to work. And I turned down overtime this week. Carley said she'd just bring a book and wait on one of the benches, but I don't feel right about it. On Monday I thought I was on time, but she was waiting outside in the heat, her face an overripe pink petunia. She wouldn't look at me, and I thought she seemed sick. She could have waited inside.

All the spots in the shade of the skimpy maples have been taken, and I know I'll hear it from Carley—that I've come inside and embarrassed her, oily-hot, wearing boots, disheveled. "Why didn't you wait in the parking lot?" she'll hiss. By then, with any luck, I'll have caught at least one staff member walking through.

"You got her back already, Miz Butler? He musta worked fast. Carley doin' okay now?"

"What?"

The aide, a hefty black woman of about forty named Donna, looks at her watch. She's wearing print scrubs and looks tired, her makeup wearing off, though she smiles at me. "Thought Carley said she probably wouldn't be back for the last group today. Dentist get the crown on that tooth?"

"She told you she had a dentist appointment?"

Donna's lips tighten and turn down. Her tone is resigned even though she phrases it as a question. "You mean she didn't? You didn't pick her up?"

"No."

"The other days? Root canal?"

"Not hardly. My God, has she been . . . ? Carley signed a contract with her social worker."

"I'm sorry. I really wasn't supposed to say. Privacy law. But I'm glad I ran into you." She puts her arm around my shoulder in a half hug and whispers, "Don't give up." Then she steps back and says,

"I'll have her social worker paged. You have a seat, please." I could almost see inside her brain: *Uh-oh. Hand this one off quick.* Donna gestures toward the chairs lining the wall. Her thighs rub, a faint sandpaper sound, as she reverses course down another hall.

In the corners of the room are faux wood tables with thumbed magazines and lamps. Shoulder-high silk ficus plants with Spanish moss at their bases stand watch in two strategic spots on the linoleum floor. Undistinguished institutional noises: the clang of a mop against a pail, an industrial sink rinsing trays on the other side of swinging doors. A woman wearing an ID comes out of the inpatient wing with a therapy dog, a chocolate Lab, tail wagging furiously. I'm about to waylay them when the loudspeaker comes on, and it makes me self-conscious as if even the dog will guess the summons is about my daughter, who's added rehab to the list of what she can't do right.

"Annie Brooks to the lobby area, please." They are seamlessly polite here, where everyone's lives are ripped and frayed. I hold myself still in the chair and wait for the tall pretty blond social worker, who's too young to have suffered her own children lying about more than how many cookies they ate. I'll bet my half of Eddie's precious house that Carley's with Roland right now. She's cooked up this story, looked her social worker, nurses, and even the most experienced aides in the eyes and lied about how I was picking her up to go to the dentist. Only it's Roland who picked her up and not to go to the dentist. He'll have her back maybe fifteen minutes before day treatment ends, and she'll sit outside to wait for me just as if she'd been here for every session. And she knows she can pull it off because no probation officer will be called if she's not here; I protected her from that. Or I protected myself.

Breathe in, breathe out, I prompt my lungs, but then I smell myself: horsey, stale sweat, and it's as if even my body is saying, *You shouldn't have come, you shouldn't know this, you don't belong here.* And that is what has happened since Carley was a child. No matter what she does, in my quietest moments, I end up feeling more wrong than she. Then the familiar inland wave rises: *Damn her. Damn him.*

Before Annie even makes it to the lobby, I am out in the parking lot. I have to do something to relieve this unbearable tightness in my chest, the pressure that threatens to explode or dissolve me. I cannot be this helpless. I know this much: Roland will be stoned, and there's one thing I can do. Hide. Wait for him to drop Carley off. Call the police with a DUI tip right before I pick her up. And hope his truck is loaded up with every poison he uses, every poison he sells.

Flies and heat and She didn't come again. The sunstruck pasture slowed. Afternoons, the herd grazed the good green grass that spread out from the back pasture fence line where the big oak, maple, and yellow poplar trees at the edge of the woods made an umbrella of shade. Undergrowth pressured the four-board fence from the tree side. The water in the ponds dropped more but was still cool from the spring that fed it.

The sound, someone coming to the house, happened often. Because it was never The Right Sound, Spice was uneasy. The day a deerfly stung the edge of his eye, his head and ears went up as he squealed, then snorted and took off in a gallop, creating a brief panic for the others. None of them had picked up danger, but now the herd spooked and moved, Charyzma breaking into a canter. All rotated their ears to listen, moved heads to look for movement, re-checked the air for the scent of a predator. None sensed anything but Spice's alarm. As he galloped toward the front pasture and barn, Spice's right front hoof came down in a burrow as he was settling down and ready to turn in a trot back to the comfort of the herd. Still, he was all right, though his eye stung and swelled. Charyzma and Moonbeam nickered to him. Afterward, the horses stayed closer together.

She didn't come. They were on their own again.

Flowers Smattered on a Tired Brown Landscape

"WE GOT TROUBLE," CAL said as soon as Eddie was in the door. "Number-one trouble."

"Do not tell me I have to take 'em back to the eye doctor. Not that it wasn't wonderful, what with your mother freakin' out when he dilated her eyes, cryin' she was blind as Hack. Getting them outta there and in the car while you were in the bar, too shit-faced blind yourself to notice that it was a cross-dresser buying your drinks." Eddie complained about it every day, still pissed off. It hadn't really been a cross-dresser, but Eddie telling Cal it had been was great revenge for being stuck with handling everything alone at the eye doctor's office. Now Cal was out of his mind about having kissed what Eddie had him convinced was definitely not a woman.

Eddie hadn't wanted to come out here today. The hours at the plant had stretched out like some damn taffy pull he couldn't get off his hands. He wanted to flop on the couch in his own air-conditioned family room with a cold beer, alone with the remote control. Instead, he'd had to go to Wal-Mart's pharmacy and pick up refills, then go to the food side and get the stuff on Cal's list.

"Oh Jesus," Cal snapped. "Shut up 'bout that. I'm talkin' 'bout the horses. Dad made me walk out to the pasture today to check on 'em again. Like I know anything, which I stupidly pointed out, so then he wanted me to bring 'em in so he could check. Managed to talk him outta that since it's a hundred fifty degrees in the shade. I think one of 'em's not walkin' right. Everything I know could be scratched on the head of a pin, except that if something happens to one of the horses and we didn't do the right thing—whatever the hell that is—we're dead men. Think we better get the vet."

"Did you tell Hack?"

"You crazy? I swore on the family Bible—well, if we had one—they were all perfect. I dunno if something's wrong. Could be. Always a big fuss about horses' legs."

"There's a problem with that vet thing. Vet's a friend of Jewel's. Patched up Carley. Did ya know that one?"

"No shit. A vet?" Cal snickered.

"I swear. Jewel's pulled off some shit, but I still can't get over that one. See . . . no police report."

"Yeah, Ed, I get it."

"Is that you, Eddie?" Louetta called from the living room, where the early news blared from the TV.

"Yeah, Lou," Eddie raised his voice, throwing it to the living room. "I brought you those sugar-free red Popsicles." Then, to Cal, ". . . speaking of which, they're probably melted."

"Jewel comin' back, Eddie?" Louetta sounded breathy, or maybe it was tired.

"Sorry, Lou."

Eddie rooted through the grocery bags on the kitchen table and crossed the kitchen in two long steps to deposit a yellow box of six Popsicles in the freezer. "I see you didn't do laundry. Isn't she out of clothes?" At the top of the basement stairs, a pile of dirty clothes languished.

"Why don't you try it? Anyway, back to that horse . . ." Cal said.

"Which one?"

Cal sighed, disgusted. "Like I'd know? A black one."

"Hey, man, I wouldn't know, either. Don't know why I asked that. Got a beer?" Even as he said it, a red flag went up in Eddie's mind. Jewel's own horse was black. He knew that much.

"Help yourself. So we get a different vet," Cal said.

"I dunno. I think they're like pediatricians or something. You don't switch around. They all know each other, too, I think. Maybe. Where's your phone book?" While Eddie went back to the refrigerator for a beer, a few bottles laid on their sides, effectively hidden in the far back on shelves behind the bulkiest groceries, Cal retrieved a phone book from under an array of dirty dishes that clanged as he moved them aside. There was no counter space uncovered.

"Hey, throw me one, too, and replace 'em, huh? They're in the broom closet, behind the vacuum cleaner. Be careful Ma doesn't see you in the hall."

Eddie traded Cal a beer for the phone book. He headed out of the room, then shrugged, came back, and used the side of one arm to clear a space on the table to set down the beer and the floppy book while he went to fetch replacement beer. He came back into the kitchen, one in each hand as if they were flowers, and hid them where the two cold ones had been.

Cal's calloused thumbs pushed off the metal cap on his beer. He stood, pondering the chaos of the kitchen, while Eddie looked under *V* in the yellow pages. "How do you spell Vet-ra-nar-ian?" Eddie asked.

"Skim through the *V* section, I guess."

Eddie closed the book, keeping his forefinger in the beginning of the *V*s as a place marker, holding it against his chest with his right hand. He pushed the heel of his left hand around the socket of his eye, pressing against his headache and the weight of his worries. "Gonna cost a fortune. Vet always costs a fortune. There's gotta be another way we can get this done," he said to his brother-in-law. "Let me think."

"Now hold up. Is that gonna smell the same as you fartin'? Care to do that outside?"

The stars had aligned for once, and volunteering to take Carley to rehab the next morning actually scored Eddie points with Jewel, like a two-for-one sale. He'd expected her to be suspicious since he'd never done it before, still pissed about Carley living with them, and then, bingo, it turned out Jewel needed the help because they gave her overtime at the office, and she was all grateful. It would definitely be a good day to buy a lottery ticket.

Eddie glanced at Carley in the passenger seat, but she kept her eyes resolutely ahead as if staring down a target. "So she caught ya, huh? How dumb was that, thinkin' you'd get away with cuttin' out of rehab? Did you get high, too?" He'd hardly spoken to her since last week when she'd done it, but now he had to.

"Buzz off."

"Well?" Eddie persisted. Holding the wheel with one hand, elbow resting on his thigh, he reached across his body with the other to flick ashes out of the open window. He wore a baseball cap with a Cincinnati Reds logo, jeans, a plain white T-shirt, and his required company ID on a lanyard around his neck. Jewel said the picture on it made him look like a felon.

Carley sighed. "Can you just leave me alone?" Her hands were clenched together, one thumb worrying the cuticles of the other hand. Chipped black nail polish. Neither short shorts nor tank tops were allowed in day treatment, so she wore jeans with large manufactured holes and a pink T-shirt that read, *I'm With Stupid.* Roland had "liberated" the shirt for Carley from a souvenir shop in Gatlinburg, outside which he'd met a connection, which was why they'd made the trip. Eddie considered the shirt an ideal summation of Carley's situation. Jewel did, too, of course; in fact, it was Jewel who'd first made the point about the shirt. *Perfect irony,* she'd called it. As he drove, Eddie had a moment of intense homesickness for how they'd once agreed about everything, how in love they'd been, her body pliant and needing him. He wanted a do-over, all the way starting from when they'd gotten married with such clarity.

Eddie jerked his thumb toward the shirt. "Your mom's right about him, y'know. She's not right about everything, but she's right about him."

Carley made a production of shifting her position in the seat to put two-thirds of her back to Eddie and look out the side window. She held her silence for a while but then said, "What're you doing? You were supposed to turn left on Marquette."

"Takin' the back way, avoidin' town. Thought you might like the scenery."

Instantly on guard. "What's going on?"

"Relax. Jesus. You'd think I was the one that shot you." He chuckled with a *sheesh* mixed into it under his breath. "Look, there's a bunch of horses out to pasture over there."

"Yeah, Eddie, this is Kentucky. The Bluegrass Region. That's what we do here." She shifted from one hip to the other.

"You used to ride and, ah, see to the horses, right?"

"What're you getting at?"

"Man, you are as paranoid as your mother. I'm just makin' conversation."

"You're full of shit."

Eddie was quiet for a good two minutes, then tried again. "So, you used to ride and stuff? Take care of . . . I mean, your mom said you did."

Carley turned and eyed him. Outside the car, pastures passed like squares of a quilt stitched with Kentucky board fences. Of course, it was Jewel who had noticed this and mentioned it, long ago, but the thought had stuck because Eddie's grandmother used to make quilts. The heads of Thoroughbreds were down, grazing. Grass shone silvery in the slant morning light. "And you're just making conversation, right?" she interrupted. She cracked her knuckles with one hand, then the other. Then she flicked her thumb up and down like the cocking mechanism of a gun. There was a small sore on it that looked like a sunset.

"Sure," he said.

"Well, let's talk about baseball, then. Who do you like for the World Series?"

"Way too early for that," Eddie said uneasily.

"Well, not really. Your Reds are out. Of course, they've been out since opening day, as usual." She was taunting him. "I like Boston, myself. Want to put a little money on anybody to make it to the series? I'll take Boston." Carley watched Eddie's face through narrowed eyes.

"Nah, not against Boston. That's like payin' you to be right," he greased the skids, having learned from Jewel how much women like to be told they're right. "So did you ever get into horseracing? The Derby and the Triple Crown stuff? Your grandfather was quite a horseman in his day, and, of course, your mother is . . ."

"Cut the shit, Eddie. I'm not stupid. What do you want?"

With great effort, Eddie resisted the temptation to respond to Carley's *I'm not stupid* comment by making reference to her shirt. Instead, he sighed deeply. He'd obviously gotten off on the wrong foot and then put the damn thing in his mouth.

"Goddammit," he said softly, shaking his head in a slow small way, sighing deeply.

"Spit it out, Eddie. And open your eyes!" She said the last loudly, grabbing the wheel and correcting the truck's trajectory as it drifted toward the right shoulder where a deep runoff ditch had been cut the year before last. Cornflowers and Queen Anne's Lace edged it now.

He controlled the wheel. "Sorry," he muttered. "Do you want something at Dunkin' Donuts?"

"Sure. But I can't be late to day treatment or they can kick me out, which would be a true heartbreak, and you'll be late to work. Don't want you blamin' me for either one."

"*Pfft*. I'm late every day." It wasn't true, not even close.

Carley shot him a look. "Why would you be late every day? That makes no sense. This is the first day you've driven me, and you only offered because Mom got overtime."

Eddie shut up. He was plain out of options. "We're five minutes to Dunkin' Donuts. We'll sit down in there, and I'll lay it out," he said.

Carley had black coffee and a chocolate-frosted donut. Eddie had two custard-filled and coffee with cream and sugar. They'd carried it all to a small booth in the back corner, and Eddie sat facing the window so he could keep an eye on his truck. It wasn't that he didn't trust people, but he preferred to be careful.

As he ate, Carley eyed him warily, waiting.

He took his time answering. "Okay," he said, licking custard from his top lip after the first donut. "Here's the deal. You want out of day treatment, is that right?"

Carley was canny. She tucked a strand of hair behind her ear, took a bite of donut, and hid her eyes from Eddie while she looked for her napkin, wiped her lips, inspected the napkin for lip gloss, and spread it out in her lap with elaborate care. "Depends on the circumstances. I'm listening."

"Uh, can I ask you not to tell your mother something? I wouldn't normally do that, but this here's, uh, different." The idea of trusting Carley made Eddie sweat in the air conditioning. He laid his cap on the battered red vinyl seat of his side of the booth and used his forearm to wipe his forehead. Grinning donuts danced on posters above his head; for the next act, he figured he'd be out in the barn, and the damn horses would be singing opera to him. That's how far gone he was, making devil's pacts with Cal and Carley.

"Wouldn't be the first time I didn't tell her something," Carley said, and he was so desperate he took that for yes. Eddie hated that she knew he wanted something; she was playing it so cool now, she might as well have slept on cucumbers.

"I just bet," Eddie said bitterly, quietly, then reined himself in. He rubbed his forehead and eyes as if he had a headache, which he did.

"Look," he said. "I have a deal to offer you. I need help. You want out of day treatment. Can you stay straight?"

"Do I look high?"

"Carley, anyone who has seventeen holes in her face pretty much always looks high to me." He gave his shrug and waited until she met his eyes before he put his hands down. "I'm not going to turn you in, so just give me an answer."

"Not seventeen," Carley said sullenly. Her hair was maybe three inches grown out now, a single bizarre light stripe over the faded black-dyed bottom. She'd taken out the eyebrow ring thanks to Jewel's nagging. "I'm straight right now. They do random pee tests in day treatment," she said finally.

"Could you stay straight? Without being locked up during the day, I mean?" Eddie studied Carley's face, and he imagined she was trying to figure his angle. It was almost funny. Now he had maybe two fingers of an upper hand. She sure had her mother's eyes, that big sky color, but her features were finer. Maybe it was that the cheekbones were higher, the skin was drawn tighter over her features, but she just had a more delicate look. When she let her hair out of the ponytail, it waved around her shoulders the way Jewel's used to at night, except for that weird two-tone thing Carley had going on.

"I just want to get back with Roland. Then I'll be outta your hair, whatever you're up to. You can tell Mom I gave you the slip, and I took money out of your wallet. She'll believe that, easy. I'll stay gone and keep quiet . . ." She looked at him, spinning it out wordlessly, offering an alternative deal.

"Not one of the options on the table. It's day treatment and the evenings chained to your mama 'n' yours truly. Or you stay one-hundred percent sober without going to rehab, and I find something else to keep you busy during the daytime instead. I drive you back and forth, and you still gotta spend the nights with us. That's the two choices. So how much do you hate day treatment, and will you keep it a secret? I mean, if I get you out of it?"

Disgust came over her face, and she started to slide out of the booth. "Gross, Eddie, if you think . . . God, you are a pig, you are . . ."

He grabbed her wrist, remembering just in time to avoid the wound on her hand, only lightly bandaged now. "Sit down. For

God's sake, Carley, I don't even want to know what's in your twisted little brain. This has to do with taking care of your grandparents. Well, not just them, really. This also has to do with the damn horses. Remember 'the beauties'?" He put quotation marks in the air with his fingers as he said the last two words with a bitter sadness.

"Oh," she said, settling back. "What's the deal?" Eddie noted she was decent enough to be flushed.

Forty minutes later, Eddie pulled the truck into his in-laws' driveway, the tires crunching on gravel and the first browning leaves of the great shade oak, ones that had lost the battle with drought. Soon enough the acorns and Osage oranges would compete for space with the gravel, and walking to the house would be a hazard.

He'd underestimated how long this all was going to take, and now he'd had to call himself off work. He'd spun a story about losing a filling, how he had to go to the dentist and would get there as soon as he could. It had been Carley's idea. It would come out of his sick time, no big loss, but it still made him uneasy. He could only do that so many times. It looked bad on a personnel record, and he was a foreman, for God's sake.

"Come on, Carley," he said. "Let's get crackin'. Fair warning. It's not pretty in there. Might not pass sanitation inspection, shall we say." He chuckled wanly as he got out of the driver's side.

Carley hesitated on her side of the truck, still holding the handle of the door. "Grandpa hates me, y'know. This isn't just coming by for an hour." Her voice was almost a whisper. She cracked her knuckles again.

"Quit doin' that, will you?" He nodded with his whole head at her hands. "Long time ago, girl. Let it go. Lotta water under the dam." He put his hand on her shoulder.

Eddie walked by Carley's side on the dirt path to the house. Hack had lined it with flagstones when he was young, but the comings and goings of years had sunk them. The grass on either side was a patchy, weedy mess, as it was in front of the house. Eddie and Cal had relied on the heat to keep it from growing, though Cal had mowed the front once, two weeks ago.

Eddie took the two steps one at a time to the back door and opened it. A finger to his lips. "Cal!" A stage whisper into the kitchen, cave-like from the brightness of the morning.

Carley peered around his shoulder. The jagged outline of dishes and boxes, like a small city on the kitchen table. Suburbs on every counter. An open loaf of bread spilling its contents. A peanut butter jar, lid off. "Holy crap," she breathed. "Has Grandma been in here?"

Eddie motioned Carley to follow him inside, again making the finger-to-lips signal for quiet. Cal lumbered into view just as they got inside the door, Carley still taking in the mess.

"They're sleepin'. Keep it down," Cal offered. He glanced at Carley. "Hey," he said in her direction. Then, to Eddie, "She doin' her thing?"

"Whatever that means," Carley said.

"Carley will take care of the horses," Eddie said slowly and deliberately to Cal, a subtext there that Carley wasn't sure of. "She's gonna see about the black one that might have a little problem, too. And help out in the house. I got something to say to both of you, and I'll just say it once so you both can hear. Carley, I'm not your mother, I'm not blind, and I'll figure it out if you're using. The first time—not the second, but the first—the deal's off, you're busted, and the truck heads back to rehab—not here—the next morning." He paused and narrowed his eyes at his brother-in-law. "Cal, you give her one joint, one beer, one anything, or you use anything when she's here, and you're outta here. And I'm meaning not one step out of line in any direction. I've got a very long memory, if you get my meaning." Eddie searched out the scar on Cal's hand and stared at it long enough to make clear that he knew its history. He was gratified to see Cal move the hand behind him, ostensibly to hook it on his waistband, as he made a show of shifting positions. Satisfied, Eddie continued. "Carley and I can handle this by ourselves. You're an extra, remember that. Don't think I can't get you gone, because I can."

Cal made a stop sign with his unscarred hand. "Whoa there. What's this? Shootout at the O-fucking-K Corral? Who died and made you God?"

"Jewel. Only she didn't die, she quit, and I'm the one that's come up with a plan that gives everybody what they want." He took a step in Cal's direction, a finger jabbing toward Cal's chest. "You got a better one?"

Cal's hand went down, but he took a step forward, glaring, though they were still a good five feet apart in the kitchen.

"Oh my God. What is this? The Middle-Aged Testosterone Show-down?" Carley drawled in a bored voice. "Why don't you cowboys either kill each other quick or back off? You're both assholes." She moved languidly to position herself between them. "Managing the horses is a piece of cake. I didn't sign on to deal with horses' asses. I can just stay in rehab if I want to be in a group with crazies. Are we doing this or not?"

It really put Eddie's boxers in a twist that his druggie stepdaugh-ter with black nail polish, striped hair, and seventeen holes in her face was right. It made him want to get rip-roaring drunk and then pass out and sleep off this whole clusterfuck for at least two or three days. Maybe then he'd wake up and poof! Jewel's psychotic break would be over, Carley and Cal would be gone. He'd know life made sense again because the hair around Jewel's face wouldn't look like the fringe on his great-grandmother's parlor curtains.

"Yeah," Eddie said, "we're doing this. Right, Cal?" He did stick an ominous undertone like a piece of log hidden in the river of his voice to float past Carley.

Cal got his drift. "Yeah," he said. "We're doin' it. I'm in."

The three of us are hungry flies in the kitchen. Eddie and Carley are crawling the cabinets for snacks while I fry burgers on the stove rather than take the time to light the grill outside.

"Mom," Carley says, "it makes no sense for Eddie to take me back and forth to rehab. Just let me have my car back."

"There's some potato salad in the fridge, if you could grab it for me," I say, and she ignores me in favor of potato chips, so I get it myself, along with lettuce and tomatoes I bought at a farm stand I pass on the way home from work. "I got us tomatoes and oops, beans too, at the stand, but the best of the season are gone. So where's Chassie again?" I ask Eddie, an effort to divert Carley with bright patter, a smattering of flowers on a tired brown landscape.

Carley's using her "start out reasonable, sound like an adult" approach. When I say no, she'll get petulant and whiny first, then she'll throw herself down Tantrum Alley. But she's not going to get to me. Eddie's offer last night to start handling Carley's transportation to and from rehab made me feel like I'd been taking some of Roland's better drugs, or Eddie had. At first, I tried to figure his angle, and then I was ashamed. Eddie was trying, and I resolved to match it; I'll be picking Rocky up at football practice for him. He's right that the timing works out better all around.

"A car would add temptation while you're in rehab. I'm proud of you, honey. Let's not make it hard for you to stick with the program," I say in my best encouraging-mother voice. Eddie transported her both ways today, and there weren't any problems. No blood on either one, for starters.

Carley's not diverted. "Temptation for what?"

I nod at the T-shirt she's wearing, a lovely job that says, *I'm With Stupid*. The shirt is the one piece of truth Roland's introduced into her life. "You can't be with him and stay sober, Carley. You know that," I say slowly, as if she's a little slow-witted.

I can almost stand back and watch the eruption coming. This must be how seismologists feel because I know what's going to happen, and yet there's nothing to be done. I busy myself turning burgers. When she doesn't say anything, I use the flat of the spatula to press the meat into the pan. It hisses and spits.

I can only stare at hamburger so long. Just as I turn around, dredging for another bit of fake cheer, Carley speaks but to Eddie instead of me.

"Don't you think it would be fine for me to have my car back, Eddie?" she says. I catch the face she's giving him, which is dark and narrow as a cave. Eddie looks uncomfortable.

"Hey," he says with a false-sounding half laugh. He leans over to scratch Copper's back and head, which lets him duck down below the line of fire. "My dog ain't in this fight. Right, Copper?"

"Right, Eddie," she says in a tone that's almost menacing. "When did you ever stay out of anything that's not your business? Should I have my car or not?"

"Hey, hey," I say. "Let's not have an uproar and just say we did. Carley, sorry, but Eddie's got no pull in this. Your contract is with me. I'm keeping the keys to that car."

"You're the one who would be in jail."

"And you were underage, drunk, and high. Anyway, our agreement is a done deal."

Eddie crosses the kitchen in three steps and sidles up next to me. He puts his arm around me, which is something he used to do in another life. "Carley," he says, and his voice is much kinder than usual, as if he's put it through a strainer to remove anger and disgust. "Give it some time. Things'll work out for you." Again, he takes me as much by surprise as if a different movie started playing in the middle of a reel. It makes me think he's accepting her living with us now.

Then he squeezes my shoulder. I kiss his cheek where the length of the day has roughened it, and he smiles.

"Sure they will, Eddie. And I know you're gonna help them work out, aren't you?" Vintage Carley.

But Eddie's gestures have drained the swamp of my cynicism and refilled it with hope. Carley stomps off with her dinner plate and plunks it in front of the TV in the family room. On a whim, because he squeezed my shoulder, instead of heading for the TV, I hold out Eddie's plate, raise my eyebrows as a question, and point to the dining room where we never eat except Thanksgiving, Christmas, and Easter. He shrugs and nods okay.

"We're going in the other room, Carley, to get away from the TV."

"Sounds excellent to me."

I put out the flowered place mats and light candles, not really for light but to show him I am meeting nice with nice, and while we eat he tells me about the production halt at the plant that made the shift manager rabid and how they'd fixed the problem in just over a half hour, which he thought was pretty good, but Crosseyed Jim was still frothing at the mouth.

We are more relaxed together than we've been in weeks. "I went out and checked on the horses the other day. That's actually how I caught Carley out of rehab. I'm usually a little late to pick her up, but since I'd taken off work to see the horses, I was early. Anyway, I had to see them, y'know? Make sure they're okay. I mean, they should be, they're pastured, but I miss them so much." I surprise myself by telling him this.

Eddie's dark eyes open, and his eyebrows go up. His mouth forms a soundless *what?* before he says, "You did? Did you, um, see your parents? I thought you wouldn't . . ."

"God, no. I told you, I'm not giving in. I parked way down at the end of the fence line and came in through the pasture. I've got to find a way to check them regularly, though. Somebody's got to be there when the farrier comes. I worry about them all the time. Maybe I can if I—"

"You didn't tell me you were going there."

"I'm telling you now. Why?"

"Are you thinking of, you know, taking your job back? Taking care of your parents?"

I sigh. Here we go again. "The agency has filled my job long ago, I'm sure. Cal is still there because my parents haven't called me, not once. They've made their choice."

Sometimes someone says something that is exactly right, whether or not it's a good idea, whether or not it will work. "Don't worry about it," he says, patting my hand. "Cal's not there forever. He'll leave, they'll call you, and maybe then you'll be willing to take your job back. I mean, I know they screwed up bad, but they are your parents. We'll get by."

I don't tell him that the agency won't just fire someone else to give me the job. For a foreman, sometimes Eddie says things that are very naive. I'm not going to start something, though; this is the first time he hasn't been all over me about how we're behind on our bills.

"How about I go check on the horses for you?" he says. "Will they bite me if I try to give them carrots for you? No reason I can't see how they're doing and take care of 'em, is there? I can be there when the furrier comes."

"Be serious. A can of creamed corn knows more about horses than you do. And it's farrier, not furrier. Which is a blacksmith. He puts shoes on horses."

"Furrier, farrier, whatever. You're always sayin' I'm not supportive. This is me. See? Supportive. You can tell me the basics, can't you? You always used to want me to get to know the horses. Yours is that black one, right? So I give her extra stuff, right?"

I laugh and take hold of his hand, the one that was patting mine. "Him. Spice is male."

"Even better. See, I'm a guy, we'll get along."

The cherry table is cool against my forearm, and I let the wood take away the heat and burden of my body as I lean forward, shaking my head in surprise. "This is so . . . nice of you. But . . . who are you, and what have you done with my husband? My husband doesn't even like horses."

Eddie mimes horror. "Don't like them, you say? Have you forgotten what a fine rider I am? I think perhaps we need to retire early so you can have a riding lesson, in fact." He withdraws his hand from mine and uses it to slowly circle my breast as he draws out the words suggestively.

Eddie's white T-shirt shows the workday, and his belly bulges at the top of his jeans. I saw these things earlier, in the better light of the kitchen, the exhaustion on his face, how he's looking older around the jowls. He could use a shave. Here, though, we're seated, and the twilight and candles are forgiving. Maybe it's making me look good to him, too. I've forgotten what it's like to make love, it's been so long. But right now I want to remember.

Creek Crossing

EDDIE FELT LIKE HE'D aged at least a year, and he, Cal, and Carley had only pulled it off for a week. On the other hand, they'd survived a week without any of them killing each other, and the old people and the horses were still alive. That was the good news. Carley was still wanting her car. It didn't help that it was sitting out in Hack and Louetta's driveway where she saw it constantly, a wreck poxed with bird droppings under the Osage orange tree. The misshapen green fruit were starting to drop on the car too, and the ones from high branches would be like falling missiles, not that anyone would notice a few more dents. But he thought he'd get Cal to help him push the car out from under the tree; Carley would probably appreciate it even if she didn't say so. Between acorns and Osage oranges, the approach to the house was a minefield in the fall.

The yard mess was nothing compared to indoors. The place was still a Red Cross disaster area because Carley had gotten into it with Cal the very first day. At least that was Eddie's best guess. When he'd arrived to fetch Carley late that afternoon, she was on a giant brown horse with a black mane and tail, riding big figure eights in the oval ring with the soft dirt. An X of hoofprints was etched in the middle. The barn, paint sporadically peeling, loomed behind it, the driveway and house to the side.

When Eddie drove in, Carley didn't even look his way. Her back and head were ruler straight, and she moved with the horse as if they were all one thing. How did she do that?

"Hey," he called from the fence, standing on the bottom rung. She didn't hear him or was ignoring him. He thought the latter was more likely. "You finished here? We gotta go."

Carley reined the horse in and jogged across the corral, stopping two feet from Eddie. The horse's head was disconcertingly close to his face now. He forced himself not to recoil, imagining she wanted to intimidate him.

"Whoa, girl. Nice. Good girl." She patted the horse's neck. "I gotta cool Charyzma down, Eddie. I gotta walk her out and brush her. And I've got to put another ice pack on Spice's leg."

"What?"

"I was pretty sure he has a bad tendon. Well, not bad, I mean strained. I got Grandpa out to check, and that's what he said. He had me cold hose it, and then he put a standing wrap on it. He thought I wouldn't remember how, but I do, I did the next one, and he checked it. Follow me into the barn, and I'll show you. I've got to give him his bute. That I didn't know, but Grandpa taught me how, which wasn't easy since Spice doesn't exactly like it, and you have to—"

Eddie made a show of looking at his watch. "What the hell are you thinking? Do you know what time it is? What can I tell your mother about where we were? You've gotta be in the house before she gets there."

"I guess if I had my car it would be my problem and I'd have to tell my own lie now, wouldn't I? But we need a vet. Grandpa says we should have an ultrasound to make sure he's—"

"Hurry it up, will you? Do they need anything from the store tomorrow?" He ignored her dig about the car and motioned toward the house with his head.

"How should I know? And did you hear me? A vet! We need a—"

"Didn't you clean up in there?" His hands went up in disgust. Talking to Carley was sand through the hourglass. It would be easier to find out from Cal. "I'll be back in a couple. Be ready, we gotta get a move on." He threw the last over his shoulder as he climbed off the fence and lumbered toward the house.

The screen door slapped behind him. Once his eyes adjusted to the lumpy disarray in the kitchen, he knew. "Cal!" he called over the noise of the television in the living room. At least Meals on Wheels had come. But the disposable food containers were piled on the table, curdling the kind of small remains Eddie and Jewel always gave to Copper. That meant Hack and Louetta had eaten the food at lunchtime instead of Cal or Carley having made them lunch and saving the Meals on Wheels for dinner, so they'd have a real dinner, like Jewel said they should. The whole system was falling apart, like a fan with blades breaking off here and there until there'd be just the center, the old people, alone in the end. His eyes watered, and he felt sick. He'd really thought he could make this work.

He sniffed and wiped his eyes with the back of his hand. "Cal!" he called again, starting into the short hallway.

His brother-in-law appeared shirtless and barefoot, thin legs poking out from beneath cutoffs. He was picking sleep from the inside corner of one eye as he shambled out. He scratched his scalp with both hands. "Yeah? Where's the fire?" he muttered. "Mom and Dad are napping, so I was, too."

Eddie pointed toward the living room. "Not hardly. They're both in there." He could see the tops of their heads. He thumbed the kitchen, behind him. "Not one thing is done out there. What the hell is going on?"

"Yeah. Carley didn't do squat, did she. Thanks a heap for the useful maid service. Spent the whole day fussing over the black horse with Dad."

Two minutes ago Eddie had been ticked off at Carley. Now he blew at Cal, gesticulating, face reddening. "Goddammit, Cal, she's out there doing exactly what she's supposed to. The horse that's got a bad leg, she's got it all iced down or something in the barn, doing what your dad told her to. She's tendin' to those horses. You're supposed to have a grocery list ready for me, check t' see if they need any medicines or anything, and get this place cleaned up. Are you high?" The last suspicion had come over him suddenly, an explanation.

Cal rolled his eyes. "Don't I wish."

Eddie stuck his face close to Cal's, trying to check his breath. He peered at Cal's eyes, not entirely sure whether he was looking for oversized pupils or tiny black stones in the pale blue pond. Cal leered back. There were dark circles under his eyes but nothing that looked weirder than the usual gape of that missing tooth.

Eddie pulled away. "Sheesh. Ever heard of a bath and a toothbrush? I'm about at the end here, man. The end. I'll give you one more day. You got something to give them for dinner?"

"Stuff in the freezer. I dunno. I been asleep. I'll look."

Eddie got out a trash bag and began clearing the table and counters of refuse. He organized the dirty dishes next to the sink since it was already full. The room was small, old-fashioned, and gloomy, but as he picked things up and moved around, Eddie felt the cabinets sticky to the touch, the linoleum floor tacky underfoot. "Jesus," he muttered, wrinkling his nose. "The place stinks. Has the floor been mopped since you've been here?" He peered out the back door. Carley was no longer in the ring. "What happened, man? She said she'd clean up in here when I dropped her off this morning. Then she was going to do the horses. You were supposed to see to the food and make a list."

"Girl's got a mouth on her."

"And you don't?" Eddie was fuming now. "Look, here's how it looks to me. She's out there working the horses. At least she's holding up some of her end. I know I'm doing my part. Right now you look entirely dispensable to this operation." He stopped where he was, a black trash bag dangling from one hand, the other hand on his hip, glaring.

Cal held up a hand. "All right, okay. Back off, already. They're gonna hear you ranting. I'll get 'em something to eat. Not time yet. Gotta eat with the pills, y'know."

"Oh really? I had no idea, Cal." Eddie's voice was thick with sarcasm. He dropped the bag on the floor. "One day you got. Think disposable. Think toilet paper, Cal. Think disposable as used toilet paper, because that's what I'm thinking. And don't think I can't get you gone." He leaned into the hallway then and followed his ear a few steps toward the television's manufactured laughter. Louetta was snoring. Cal had been right about that much, but Eddie was unmollified.

He left through the kitchen door saying, "Have a damn list ready for me when I show up with Carley tomorrow. And check to see what cleaning supplies you need." To the extent that a bear can stalk, Eddie stalked across the side yard toward the barn. None of the horses was in sight. Carley must have finished with the big brown horse and turned all of them back out to pasture.

The large barn doors were open, which meant Carley was inside. He crossed in front of his truck and went in, his eyes having to adjust all over again. When he looked down the center aisle, he saw that she had the black horse, Jewel's, in one of the stalls and was inside with him, crooning. The sound made him unaccountably angry, riled up still and again.

He threw his voice to the stall. "Goddammit, Carley, we gotta go. And tomorrow that house better get cleaned up."

"I can't leave Spice yet," she called back over the door. "Come look. Well, you can't see because I've got a polo wrap over the ice pack now, but he's got a little bit of heat and swelling on his tendon, right here, right foreleg. It's got to stay on for twenty minutes, and then I just need to redo the standing wrap." Her voice muffled as she bent over again. "Grandpa says Red had this happen once and other horses he trained. We're giving him bute, that's like horse aspirin. Oh, I told you that already. We've got a supply. Grandpa and Mom keep it in the barn. Grandpa said to put him on stall rest, and I'll have to keep doing the cold hose on it and the bute for almost two weeks, and then I start walking him on a lead rope. Grandpa says it's not bad, but we should have a vet 'cause it's Mom's horse. Come see . . ." She stood and gestured over the stall door, a wave forward. "Grandpa thinks he either stepped in a hole or he was just romping in the field on his own—"

She sounded just like her mother with the annoying horse jargon that normal people don't know and don't want to. Eddie cut her off. "What don't you get, girl? We have to go. Your mother . . ."

Still standing, her voice edged with belligerence now. "My mother would shit a brick if she knew her horse was hurt, and you know it. I need the vet to look at him. They've got portable ultrasounds, see—"

Just hearing her say the word *ultrasound* made Eddie sweat. He'd been married to Jewel long enough to have some idea of what horse vets cost. "No vet. You think I'm made of cash? You said it's not bad. Hack can tell you what to do." He tapped his watch with the forefinger of his other hand, glaring his impatience.

The black horse made a soft snortlike sound. Eddie saw a bobbing movement behind Carley, and her arm, pale in the musky light of the barn, went up and caught something. Eddie took steps forward until he distinguished the horse's head and red halter in the dark recess of the barn.

"It's okay, boy, okay, okay. I'm here. I'm right here," Carley said, her face against the horse's, her arm on his neck. Eddie could scarcely make out the words; it was another voice entirely than the one she used to him, one he'd not heard from the girl before. Gentle. Kind. Unhurried. It set him off. Goddamn, he'd clocked out instead of staying to fix the broken gear, leaving his boss mad at him, all to keep this house of cards standing up.

"Carley! Now!"

She almost roared out of the stall, the wooden door banging back on its hinge as if Carley herself were a small explosive device. Eddie saw the horse startle against some sort of rope contraption.

"I told you. I can't leave right now. I need to leave this ice pack on for at least twenty more minutes. Go call Mom. Make up whatever lie you want." As she approached, Carley's voice got louder. "Tell her we're riding go-carts and bonding. Tell her that I have you at gunpoint because you're too dumb to live. I don't care what you tell her. I'm not leaving yet."

"The horse can wait until tomorrow morning."

"I am not going to fuck up taking care of my mother's horse."

"So now you owe your mother? Last I knew, you were barely speaking to her. I'm the one got you out of rehab, remember?"

"Get me my car, and maybe we'll talk about how goddamn much you do for me." Carley spit the words, her neck red.

Eddie wanted to lash her, and he couldn't have said why. It had something to do with hearing her soothe the horse. She'd never had one kind word for him, a damn decent stepfather. At least he'd tried, unlike her real father. "I'll tell you one thing," he growled. "You're so hot for the keys to your car so you can sneak off to see Roland The Stupid, but uh-oh. Too bad. Your mother called the cops on your personal drug lord right after he took you on your little junket-from-rehab. It's not like you weren't warned." Eddie chuckled for effect, ignoring Carley's widening eyes, how her mouth was opening in a child's shock. "Yep, she tracks his residence in jail with great delight on the Internet. You didn't think anybody would post bail, did you? Bet you've had a bit of trouble reaching him."

He didn't even have time to react. Carley threw herself at him in a rage, pummeling and sobbing, shouting, "Bastard! Fucking bastard liar!" Eddie staggered backward, unprepared. Her weight wasn't enough to knock him over, but she did land several good blows. There was noise in the stall, something banging.

"Quit, quit," Eddie yelled, fending her off.

Then someone else was there, pulling Carley off him. Cal. He put himself between Eddie and Carley, with his back to Eddie, holding his niece's shoulders. "Hey, hey, girl, whatsa matter? Settle down."

Carley tried to jerk away. "Liar," she shouted at Eddie.

"Ask her," Eddie retorted.

"Will you two stop shouting? Even *I* can tell the horse is getting worked up," Cal said.

Carley looked over her shoulder to see the gelding's head straining against the crosstie, the whites of his eyes visible. She wrenched herself from Cal's grip and hurried to the stall. "Whoa, boy," she said softly, opening the door and taking hold of the halter. "Easy now. You're fine. I'm sorry, boy. Easy. Okay, you're okay. Good boy, easy, easy." As she spoke, she stroked the horse's neck. Eddie heard that she was crying.

Cal slugged Eddie's bicep, not hard, and gestured with his head, meaning *outside*. Eddie pointed to his watch, as he had to Carley, and put his palms up for emphasis but followed Cal out the wide barn doors into the thinning autumn afternoon. Their shadows led them.

"So," Cal turned once they were clear of the barn, using righteous indignation to get in Eddie's face. "According to you, I'm disposable as used toilet paper, and Miss Carley is Miss Perfect, but two minutes later, I hear her screeching like a banshee and I have to tear out to break up a fistfight. And buddy, I think she coulda taken you out."

Lecturing, Cal looked plain ridiculous, still shirtless, slack fat resting on top of the waist of his denim cutoffs. The rake-handle legs under the heft of his torso were bad enough, but, worse, he'd stuffed his feet into Louetta's scuff slippers, very pink, with fluff over the top.

Eddie wanted to stay worked up for the energy to get himself and Carley back home to Jewel on some sort of schedule. He was the engine of this operation.

He just couldn't. Laughter began from inside him, and, once started, his laughter took hold, gathering up and smothering his every other thought. Cal's eyes widened, then narrowed as Eddie completely lost control, tears coming from his eyes. Shaking his head, he took a step toward the barn.

"No way. Leave her alone." Cal blocked his way.

Head down to wipe his eyes on his shirt, Eddie got a fresh look at Cal's feet and broke up all over again. Hardly able to speak, and with Cal still glowering at him, Eddie choked out the words. "Okay, man. *You* go in there. Tell Carley . . . tell Carley I said I'm sorry. Tell her t' take the time she needs with the horse. I'll call Jewel like she said and make something up about why we're late. Tell her I'm sorry."

"Idiot," Cal muttered and went into the barn. Eddie headed to the house, still chuckling. If he left a message on the answering machine at home instead of calling her cell phone, then he could avoid talking to Jewel directly. He mopped his face with his hand and was surprised to find how wet it was. He'd intended to go into the house to snag one of Cal's buried beers, but when he realized he was crying and could no more stop his rough sobs than he'd been able to stop his laughter, he was too embarrassed to risk Cal or one of his in-laws seeing him and continued to the far side of the house to hide.

The herd was happier for the attention but unsettled. Someone was coming every day, someone who looked and sounded like Her but wasn't. Charyzma best remembered the girl who came, though Red remembered her, too. They took to her most easily, even though she'd touched the others, and each of them had carried her in the past. But the girl hadn't been around in a long time, and, suddenly, before the grass was dry every morning, the heavier, different sound on the gravel was there, and so was she. Moonbeam was calmest because the girl brought the old man to her. The first day, the old man laid his head on Moonie's withers, an arm over her black-over-white-spotted back. Moonie felt the frail weight and didn't step until the girl moved the old man to a chair.

But She still didn't come, and the girl had taken Spice away. The herd grazed behind the corral in the front pasture because Spice called to them and they to him. The pasture was sun-eaten there, nothing tall or sweet. Often the girl brought them into the corral to hose them with cool water. She filled buckets because they weren't near the small pond and rode them all except Spice in the big ring. Spice whinnied to them from where he was kept, and they answered, *yes, I am still here, yes, here I am too, yes, yes.*

———————

Carley hadn't worried about whether she remembered how to take care of the horses. No matter how long it's been since you mucked a stall, cleaned hooves, wielded a curry brush, tightened a girth, and threw your leg over the seat of a saddle, *how* isn't something you forget. What she had forgotten was the *why*. By September every bit of it had come back.

"Hey, good girl, come on sweet stuff, open your mouth for Mama," she said. No need to feel foolish when no one but Charyzma could hear. The mare's ears flicked, listening, as Carley's fingers pressed on the sides of her mouth. "There's my girl. I saved the best for last today. We've got time to do a little jumping. Have some fun, you and me." The bit slid into place over Charyzma's tongue, and Carley slid the leather bridle over her ears. Hack was already waiting for them at the riding ring; after he checked Spice each day, he wanted to stay out in one of the chairs she'd set up for him in the barn, by the corral, or just outside the ring, and Carley was amazed at how much her grandfather knew.

She'd already spent an hour working with Spice, walking him. He could be turned out in the corral now, her grandfather said. No sign of any lameness, but they'd have to be careful for a long time. A strained tendon was nothing to fool with. Since Crazy Eddie had nixed calling a vet, she'd spent the weeks meticulously cold hosing and wrapping his foreleg, and if she'd taken her grandfather in for his nap, she'd talk to the horse while she did, which was strangely comforting. Even though her grandfather couldn't see what she was doing, she cleaned the gelding's stall daily and put down fresh straw. Once he said, "Jewel couldn't do a better job with that horse herself," and she'd tucked the words away to examine later. Did he really mean such praise for her?

"Your mother send you to take care of things?" he said. "Your grandmother's been sure she'll come back herself. You know anything about that happening soon?"

"Not really, Grandpa. But remember, she's had me come take care of chores before. It's, you know, it's Cal. Don't worry, though. Between you and me, we've got everything covered with the horses."

Keeping Spice stalled meant they'd had to buy hay and a hundred pounds of grain because the barrel was nearly empty. "We'd have to buy it by November anyway," Carley said to Eddie. "How long do you think they can live off pasture? There's this little thing called winter."

Eddie paid for the hay and grain because Spice was Jewel's horse. When the others needed it, too, Hack would pay for their feed, but starting one horse on hay and grain was a harbinger of the time all four would need grain, hay thrown twice a day, their stalls mucked when they couldn't be out, lunge exercise when weather wouldn't permit riding. The damn winter. Carley knew Eddie was brooding on it, too, and she knew why. "Your mother will be fussing about the horses," he said. "Well, she already is. Except I tell her I'm checking on them for her, and she likes that. But winter's the thing. She's tryin' to figure out what to do about the horses, y'know, while she's got her boycott thing goin' on. I gotta figure out how to head her off. Fresh outta ideas."

They were in Eddie's truck on the way home at the time, Carley sweaty, her hair escaping from where she'd pinned it back. She'd changed back into the clean clothes she'd worn that morning, but not left herself enough time to wash the horsey smell off herself before Eddie picked her up. Now she kept barn clothes at her grandparents' house, and Cal put them in the wash at night. Some things would have clued Jewel in right away. She'd been wearing a pair of her mother's boots to avoid manure on her shoes; there were two pair, stiff and cobwebbed, in the tack room. Carley had picked the pair with the least cracked leather, cleaned and softened them with saddle soap. Putting on broken-in boots gave her a sense of going to work—a sense she remembered from her childhood—but besides dodging her mother's eyes and nose, no self-respecting horse person wore shoes in a barn.

Carley stared out of the passenger side window for a minute then, trying to wrap her mind around what her stepfather was saying. October was announcing its arrival; yes, pastures were still green, and horses out everywhere, their heads down to the grass. Charyzma's flying lead changes were much crisper and more balanced since they'd been working. That horse could do anything: go Western or English, and Carley had started her jumping again. Carley's grandfather was teaching her advanced training techniques now; the horses were sharpening old moves, learning new ones. The herd hated being separated. She wanted them fully reunited, and Spice nearly ready for light workouts. She didn't know if her mother would accept it if she trained him, but Carley was sure she could. Still, look how much earlier twilight came, and all this yellow and burnt orange splashed onto the treetops.

Eddie was saying he didn't see how to keep this going, wasn't he? Carley twisted sadness to irritation. "What are *you* gettin' out of this, Eddie?"

"I'm trying t' keep a family together."

She narrowed her eyes and nodded, "Right," she said, drawing the word out like taffy.

He'd been at work all day, and he didn't smell the best. His T-shirt had dirt on it. He looked older than Carley thought he was with those circles under his eyes and what looked like sprinkles of silver in his buzz cut, but that could have been the light.

"Jesus. Cut me some slack, Carley. I'm keeping your grandparents out of a nursing home."

"Okay," she answered, with a shrug to cut him off. She wanted a shower and something to eat, not to listen to Eddie blather. She just wanted to get back to her horses tomorrow; taking Charyzma over low jumps as part of her workout was exhilarating. She wasn't in rehab, but she *was* rock sober, which was turning out all right. Fine, in fact. She still loved Roland, and she hadn't forgiven her mother, but there wasn't anything she could do to get him out of jail without money or a car. She *should* be chomping at the bit, working on some elaborate plan to help Roland—who must still think she was in rehab—but in truth, if this arrangement went on forever it would be dandy with her. She didn't want things to change, which felt like a dirty, disloyal secret. She and Cal had settled in, weird as it was, each with fenced-off areas of responsibility. He was sober in the mornings, and that was when she talked to him. Even her grandfather thought she was doing a good job. She'd take him out to the barn, and he'd run his gnarled hand down Spice's leg and listen intently for any irregular sound as she led her mother's horse around the paddock to keep good blood circulation to his legs, her grandfather said. Then he'd want to stay to help brush each horse and clean hooves while they talked about the horses and he gave her training advice and warning signs of colic, ringworm, mud fever, sweet itch, laminitis. "Make sure you're always checking for cracked heels," he said. "I drilled that into Jewel."

"Yeah, I remember that, but I want to organize it all," she said and asked Eddie to buy her a notebook when he did the shopping.

"Not bad. Not bad at all," her grandfather said to her one day after he'd sat by the ring listening to the tempo of hoofbeats, her own voice woven between them, as she worked Charyzma. "Well done. Maybe we should think about buying a yearling."

"What? Really?"

"No. Gotta be at least eighteen months, goin' on two. But you need to know how to train up a baby."

It was Friday, a week after Eddie had said the business about *keeping your grandparents out of a nursing home*, and the land was an ache of beauty. Too dry still, but a midweek cold snap had come and gone, and the burning bushes to the side of the house had ignited scarlet. The trees edging the back pasture were holding two thoughts, summer and full autumn, and seemed to love them equally under an intense blue sky.

In jeans, a long-sleeved T-shirt, and a cowboy hat she'd last worn in 4-H, Carley saddled Red for an afternoon trail ride. Red deserved it, she rationalized, because he was the most reliable, though she knew she loved him and Charyzma specially. The barn chores were finished, and the other horses, except Spice, were turned out to graze. Spice was in his stall, outfitted with a cold pack that would last about thirty minutes as it warmed to air temperature. When he checked the tendon yesterday, her grandpa confirmed that she should start to exercise him a little more. They decided that for the first week of that unless she cold-hosed the leg for twenty minutes, she'd stall him and put a cold pack on the leg after the exercise just to be over-cautious. Probably that was more than a vet would have had them do, her grandfather said. "I've treated these mild strains myself for years, y'know. Don't get why Eddie wouldn't have Summer come check him, though. She's a good vet. I'd have thought he'd have called her. Just 'cause it's your mother's horse." Exactly the problem, Carley thought. My mother.

Carley had loved the old trails as a child. One, wider than the rest, was the remnant of an old wagon lane that the first settlers had created. "Sure, this was pioneer land," Carley remembered Jewel telling her years ago. "Probably they brought our bluegrass, honey. But it spreads so fast, it might have beat the settlers here. Lotta people think it's native to Kentucky, but it's not. Your grandpa told me." Jewel used to drop tidbits like this all the time, ones that lately surfaced in Carley's mind at the most unexpected times. "The seeds were on horses' hooves and then on wagon wheels, and it spread as the travelers came. Some people even spread bluegrass seed along the trail so that when their relatives followed them west, their horses would have something to eat." Not many people had woods with old pioneer roads anymore; a lot of land that wasn't active pasture had gone to developers. Long ago Jewel had told her that when her grandparents died, the house and barn and land might have to be sold, something she hadn't cared about at all when she'd heard it but now it gave her a sick feeling. Sometimes Carley had a brief sense of what had been lost and the losses to come. Then a flat heavy river rock of sadness and desire pressed on her chest, and she did not want to think about it.

The other horses had been edgy when Carley kept Red in the corral to saddle him, and they stayed nearby in the front pasture. When Red was under saddle and Carley rode out, all of their heads were up, watching, ears ticked toward Red. Charyzma nickered to him, and Red gave a quiet answer. It wasn't enough. The horses trailed them to the back pasture. They'd stay there, probably near the big pond where the grass was tall and deep green, until she and Red returned, then follow them in again.

The trail was obscure. Carley didn't know if it was from disuse or because more leaves had fallen than she thought; they were still soft, yellow, not brown, and the light in the woods was yellow, too. Red's hooves made a soft swishing thud in them, his tail flicking occasionally. "Good boy, you know the way," she said, patting his neck frequently, carrying on a conversation to which Red attended, tipping his ears back to pick up her voice. "What do you think, boy? Wanna cross the creek? Have you missed our trail rides? Oh God, remember that time we tried barrel racing? Fourth place wasn't that bad. Okay, so there were only five kids in it. Yeah, that last one was disqualified, but it was our first time. We should've tried again. Kentucky's not exactly a rodeo state, but it was cool. That's what you're built for, not that sissy dressage stuff. Let Charyzma do that, huh?"

Carley reached to stroke Red's neck, the wound on her hand healed over but still outlined in a slightly puffy pink. She saw it, isolated that way, and chose not to think about it, instead talking on to Red as she rode the downhill trail to the creek, letting him stay in a leisurely walk. Carley automatically leaned back in the saddle to distribute her weight whenever there was a steep decline. Red's white socks flashed above his hooves, steady, picking his way. "Roland's never even been on a horse," she confided to Red. "He'd call me a certified redneck right now." Her sex with Roland had been bawdy and fun, except the times one or both of them had been too wasted. One time his mouth and hands had been tender—none of the rowdy ass-slapping and devouring teeth—after he'd told her things from his childhood that he'd not put into words before—and he'd cried. She'd held him and he'd cried.

"But I don't see him ever getting a real job, Red. Talk about making reservations. He'll be high twenty minutes after he's out." Carley shook her head. "God, listen to me, boy. Do I sound like one of those rehab suck-ups or what? Like Miss Pamela Goodie-Goodie." Carley tried to laugh at herself as she leaned forward to caress Red's neck with her free hand. She rode a Western saddle, long loose reins in her left hand, and her back was supple as she leaned far over the saddle horn in an expansive, affectionate gesture with her right.

She overreached just enough to affect her balance in the saddle.
Her heels came up, and she pitched forward, upper body over Red's
withers and crest, face into his mane. She had a decent grip with
her thighs and knees, so though her butt pitched up, she stayed on.
But Carley knew she'd made a dumb mistake that could have been
dangerous with a less reliable horse, one that would have startled
or bolted. She tightened up on the reins as best she could with her
left hand but had to rely on Red's recognition of voice commands.
"Whoa, boy, whoa. Stand," she said, keeping her voice calm, and
Red did, stopping dead on the trail. Carley, the saddle horn digging
into her gut, laid her head on Red's neck and cried.

"It's a damn good thing *you're* not a druggie, Red. I'd be flat on
my ass. With a broken leg. And you'd have run a mile ahead by now.
I love you, boy," she said.

She gave herself perhaps three or four minutes to cry, repeating
"stand" once when Red took a questioning half step, and, responding,
the horse remained in place. Carley's feet were out of the stirrups,
and she'd wrapped the reins loosely around the horn, no pressure
on the bit.

"Okay, boy, I'm okay now," she said finally, sitting upright in the
saddle again, wiping her eyes with the back of her hand. "I just want
to be as good as you." Carley took up the reins and signaled Red to
walk with the pressure of her calves and heels. "Walk on." She reined
him around toward the trail to the creek, where this time of year the
water would shine clean as light. When Red turned, the long white
blaze on his face was visible and the reddish-brown forelock against
it that was beautiful to her. "Walk on, walk on," she whispered to the
horse, the first command she'd learned when her mother taught her
to ride. Then she'd learned those words in a song in sixth grade, and
the words reminded her of the creek, how the clean hopeful water
always came to them from somewhere unknown and mysterious
and then kept on its way, again and again and again.

After Red had a drink in the creek, there was a flat area on the
way back where they could canter together, which is what it felt like
to Carley, more than asking the horse to run. It was always what
they did together: she'd signal him which lead to pick up by leaning
ever so slightly toward his inside shoulder and pressuring lightly

with the opposite heel. Her thighs would cling, and then their motions would mirror one another.

Maybe they'd flatten out into a brief full-out gallop. Then he'd have plenty of time to cool down on the way home. She knew what to do.

The sun was a skirt over the tree-tops when Carley reached the back pasture gate. She was fine for time; all she had to do was ride Red to the barn, unsaddle, brush him down, pick out his feet, and turn him loose. She'd still have time to clean herself up and be ready when Eddie came to get her. She dismounted and dragged open the ancient gate, led Red through, and latched it behind them. Remounted, she let Red pick up a slow jog toward the barn, scanning pasture, pond, and run-in shelter for the other horses as they went along.

None were in sight. Carley's eyes narrowed, and prickles of unease rose along her arms as if the wind had shifted, carrying weather, which it hadn't. It made no sense. No way had Cal called those horses in, nor Eddie. Her grandfather? No way. He relied on her to take him out of the house. *Oh my God*, Carley thought, panicked. *Mom's here. And she's gotta be looking for Red. I'm so busted.*

She pulled Red up short. He was cool; that was good. It was worth a try. She dismounted, uncinched the saddle, and pulled it off him. She used the saddle blanket to rough his coat the wrong direction. About twelve feet away there was a bare spot on the ground, and from it she got some dirt to rub on him in several places. Maybe if Jewel hadn't been there long, she'd think Red had just found a nice spot and decided to roll. He was one to do that more than the others. Probably, though, her mother was frantic and on her way out here right now. She might well be saddling one of the other horses or, more likely, would just climb on bareback if Red didn't come in.

Carley slid the bit out of Red's mouth and lifted the bridle over his ears, setting him free. She slapped his rump to encourage him. "Get going, boy. Go home, go home!" she said, flapping her arms at him. "Go on!"

Red startled and cantered a few steps but then hesitated, slowing to a trot. He looked back at Carley. "Go on, get home boy!" she shouted, flapping her arms again, and he turned and headed home.

I told Helen in personnel I had a migraine and had to leave early today. I lose a day of overtime, but I've got to see the horses, be with them again. On his way out this morning, Eddie said he and Carley would likely be late getting home after he picks her up at rehab. He wants to go get parts for his truck so he can spend Saturday morning working on it. I didn't say anything, not wanting to make him feel bad, but my first thought was that he won't have time to go out and check the horses today if they're going to the Truck Supply.

I have no confrontation in mind. The more I've thought about it, the more I expect to be completely ignored—if I'm even seen. I parked on the road and slipped into the barn by coming around from the side away from the house. I've got to check what grain there is, whether it's getting moldy, and how much straw is left for bedding. October has begun. Somebody's got to think about these things. Probably we can order hay from Pelley's again; it was good last year, lots of alfalfa in it. Who else is going to do this?

It's not that Eddie's word hasn't been gold about checking the horses. "All there and healthy-looking," he says regularly. "Nope, no one showed a face out of the house. I just parked on the road again and kept to myself." It's way better than nothing, but beyond knowing a dead horse from a live one, giving the carrots and apples I load him up with, petting the horses and talking to them, and reassuring me that no horse is limping or showing other signs of distress, Eddie isn't a lot of use. I can't tell him how to groom, clean feet, sniff out moldy grain, or tell how much more straw we'll need. I can't expect him to throw the hay and scoop the grain all winter, let alone when to stall the horses and when to turn them out. He doesn't even know how to put on a halter; I can't tell him how to do that, even though he wants me to try. But Eddie can't possibly be enough; the horses need me. Still, seeing his determination to help me is like turning over a stone in a stream, one that looked disappointing on the surface and then underneath you find a much deeper color, something to amaze you.

And another good has come of Eddie's looking in on the horses for me: it's shown me that if he can just go fool with the horses and be completely ignored, I might well be able to pull off the same thing.

I sense his presence before I hear him, and before my eyes adjust to the dimness of the barn I hear the soft thump of his hoof as he steps within the stall. Spice. I am startled, and more, frightened. Who here could have, would have, brought my horse in, and why? I hurry down the center of the barn to his door, calling to him, working to keep my voice quiet and unalarmed. "Hey, boy, my beautiful boy. What're you doing in here? Are you all right?" As soon as I open the door, I see that his leg has a cold pack on it. My mind is a rush hour of questions honking their horns.

"Are you hurt, boy? What happened?" My face against his, arms around his neck. Squatting, I remove the pack, which isn't cold, just faintly cool, to examine his leg. It's not swollen, no heat. No cut, nothing I can see. I put on his halter, taking it from its nail outside the door, and lead him out. Automatically I check: yes, his stall has been mucked, the straw is fresh, and the watering system is working. As I walk Spice up and down the center of the barn, I don't see any hitch in his step. He looks completely sound to me. "Okay, boy, I'll check the others and then get back to you." I put him back, for which I get a small snort. He wants out.

In the feed area, there's fresh grain in the barrel and four bales of hay. But Spice can't have been stalled for more than a couple of days, or Eddie would have seen and told me. I grab the pail and put a good scoop of grain in it, take three halters, and, to keep myself small and unnoticed, use the back door out of the barn to find the others.

From just behind the corral fence on the side away from the house, I try bringing them in using my rings on the metal pail and whistling. If they're in the back pasture, I may have to leave the grain here, walk out with carrots, and call their names.

But Moonie's head appears over the rise. She's in no big hurry, but she's coming. Usually it's Charyzma in the lead. Now she comes, too, a length behind Moonbeam and closing in. I cannot see them without smiling. "Well, come on, you two lazy girls," I sing out, waving the pail around. "I've got you some grain. Where's Red?" The horses expand my heart every time I'm with them.

Moonie picks up the pace, her face like a sunflower bending toward me now. She's recognized my voice. Within minutes we are having a reunion. "Save some for Red." I laugh as they crowd each other at the fence for the grain, which I'm scooping out to hand-feed with both hands, palms flat. They look good, much cleaner than I expected after not being regularly groomed. But Dad must have been trying to do it. "You two are something. Bet your feet can use cleaning, though." I reach to my rear. No back pocket, no hoof pick. I'm still in the khaki pants I wore to the office though I've got on the boots from the trunk of my car; today's was a last minute plan.

And where's Red? As I make my way to the gate to bring them in, Moonbeam and Charyzma following along the corral fence, eager for more grain and, I'd like to think, my attention, there's still no sign of him. What if he's sick or injured in the back pasture? Colic? Stepped in a hole and broken his leg? But somebody put a cold pack on Spice's leg, I tell myself. What's going on?

I have to check. I leave Charyzma and Moonbeam in the pasture and go back into the far side of the barn for a bridle. I'll ride Moonie bareback to look for Red. She's the smaller of those two, and I can use the fence for a leg up onto her.

The sky is almost turquoise, and the air is good, cool, with that leafy golden edge of fall in it. I can almost feel the earth turning, and my heart wants to be happy that I'm going to ride, no matter the reason. With Moonie's bridle slung over my shoulder, I'm back out of the barn and on the way to get her when I hear what I'd convinced myself I wouldn't.

"Yo! Jewel!"

"What, Cal?" He's approaching out of the house fast, at an angle that cuts me off from the horses. And, oh my God, he's got on Mama's pink bedroom slippers, his heels hanging over the backs. "Nice shoes," I add.

"Yeah, well, I dress up formal for company." He dares to grin at me. "So . . . you, ah, come to . . . visit . . . or something?"

"Or *something*. What's going on with my horse? Who put him in his stall and *why*?"

At first Cal's face registers a blank, but seconds later, he says, "Oh, yeah, that one's yours. I did it. I been taking care of him. You know, *somebody's* got to."

"You?"

"Yeah, me."

"For God's sake, Cal, what do you know about horses?"

"More than you'd think. Can't grow up around Dad and not pick up a little something. But he's been tellin' me what t' do. Thought your horse might have a small, small problem, and Dad said to put him in the stall. All there was to it."

"And Dad told you to put a cold pack on his leg?"

"Yep."

"And told you how to do it?"

"Shit, Jewel, Dad did that part, but how hard is it anyway?"

"What's wrong with his leg?

"Turns out nothing's wrong. Dad just checked it and said turns out it wasn't nothing at all. A bee sting or something like that, he said. Supposed to let him out anyway. Dad's been checkin' all the horses."

"How does he get them in?"

"Makes me do it."

"You cleaned his stall?"

"Just put him in it. Don't wanna, don't hafta. Supposed to let him out."

"You fed him?"

"Listen, Dad sat there, told me everything to do."

"And you got the hay and grain?"

"Dad said who to call and what to say. Said he needed it anyway."

I am in a rage, the image of Cal and Carley in the stall indelible. "I don't want you touching him or anything else that's mine. I checked his leg, I'll check it again. I'll have my vet—"

"Not necessary. A bee sting is all it was. Dad says he's fine. All of 'em are good."

Cal looks out toward the pasture. My eyes follow his. "Red's not with the other two," I say. "Have you seen him today since you're so suddenly *responsible*."

"Jesus, Jewel," he says softly. "I thought you might be glad. That I was takin' care of 'em, I mean. I'm doin' the best I can here." The breeze takes his hair, long and stringy and patchy-thin, and blows it across his face. The hand he uses to brush it out of his eyes is still scarred, a flat white statement like the tone I take with him.

"The best you can, Cal? Now that's one pathetic standard. Remember how you got that scar?" I tap my front teeth. "I only wish my daughter had the same sense. And that she hadn't deflected my bullet."

Cal puts his head down. "Carley's of age," he says. "Her idea. And . . . we were wasted."

"I suppose it was my idea back then."

He shakes his head.

"Look at me."

Cal seems to drag his head off his chest and finally meets my eyes. "You hurt me. You were no brother. Now you've hurt my daughter—not that she's smart enough to know it. I know you don't care, but I won't ever forgive you."

Cal does the one thing he could that would surprise me. "I care," he says, eyes up, and it seems he's about to say more. But something behind me diverts him. "Hey, there's the horse you were askin' about, right? Told you he was fine," Cal says, pointing well beyond where Charyzma and Moonie are grazing patiently near the fence in the foreground.

I turn, and, yes, Red is on the crest, coming in on his own. Cal seems relieved. "Just so you know, Mom and Dad are doin' fine. The agency people are workin' out good," he says and turns to go back into the house, the heels of Mama's fluffy pink slippers flapping, entirely ridiculous, something I wish I could fall to my knees laughing at until I finally cry.

Through the Looking Glass

CARLEY HAD NO IDEA how long to wait out in the back pasture. Thank God Eddie told her mom they'd be late tonight. He'd made up a story about looking for truck parts because they needed to grocery shop for her grandparents. The list she and Cal had made was waiting on the kitchen counter. *Oh crap, it was in her handwriting, would Mom go into the house?* The thought was an anxious rush as complications spread like a brush fire. Was anything of hers lying around? Everything depended on whether Cal was quick on his feet and thought to stash everything fast if her mother came to the door. On the other hand, what was she thinking? Her grandparents would mention *Eddie* and *Carley* to Jewel if she came into the house. They had no reason not to. Unless they were sleeping. Unless Cal could head them off.

No, there'd be a nuclear explosion if her mother went into the house.

Why was her mother here, anyway?

Carley hiked around the back pasture for what she guessed was well over an hour. At first she'd tried sitting, a fence post tattooing itself into her back, but she was too nervous to stay still. She was noticing first signs of twilight, ground colors starting to fade and darken, though the sky and treetops still held plenty of light and color, thanks to Daylight Saving Time. She was getting cold, though. No one came looking for her, which she took as a good sign. Sending Red to the barn might have worked, but, on the other hand, it might mean Jewel was waiting to ambush her. And if that was the case, her mother would wait forever. The crickets were in full throttle now. Eddie would be showing up at the house any minute. She had to at least get close enough to see what was in the driveway.

She moved the saddle and bridle to the most protected place, against the fence where goldenrod and asters were luminous as they clung to the memory of sun. She covered the tack with Red's saddle blanket. *I can do this*, she told herself and headed for the barn.

By walking slowly, she gave darkness time to rise higher off the ground. A breathy barred owl called, *hoo-hoo-hoohoo*. She stuck to the same fence line, the one that went by the far side of the corral and barn, past the riding ring, and out to the road, trying to make her body small and unobtrusive. Several bats swooped, not far enough overhead. When she got closer, Carley discerned Eddie's truck, habitually parked as close to the house as possible to avoid an extra ten or twelve steps.

The horses were all grazing in the front pasture, including Spice. Dammit. That meant she must have been right about her mother, and another dammit, because Carley hadn't been planning to turn him out with the others yet. She'd nursed that leg *so* carefully. But aside from that, were they busted?

She quietly edged open the back door of the barn. Her heart was too noisy. She strained to hear whether she was alone.

The darkness inside was almost complete. Only ambient light from the tack room window helped her make her way down the center aisle. Surely no one was doing anything in here. Still, she was as frightened as she'd ever been. She crossed the barn floor hurriedly and slipped out the tack room door, Eddie's truck blocking the view of anyone looking out from the house.

The kitchen window was open several inches, as it always was now. Cal kept it that way so he could exhale smoke outdoors. When Eddie was there, he did it, too, leaning over the sink and twisting his neck to the side above it, like some odd bit of plumbing, so he could aim it through the gap. There was fluid in Grandma's legs, the doctor had said, and now she had to use oxygen at night. Once in a while during the day, too, depending on whether she was having trouble breathing. *No smoking anywhere around her*, he'd apparently lectured Cal, who'd come out and passed it on to Eddie, slouched and bored in the waiting room. They weren't cheerful about it. (Twice already the wind had been wrong, of course, and it had come right back in their faces, something it shouldn't have taken a rocket scientist to realize would happen, since the ancient curtains were flapping into the room. Carley had seen what was coming and hadn't said anything so she could laugh and call them Dumb and Dumber again.)

She picked her way across the gravel and then ducked and ran over the weedy grass. She could see the top of Eddie's head though the kitchen window, but that was all. Jewel could be in there, too, for all she knew, and, if so, it was a place to avoid.

There were overgrown bushes along the side of the house, and Carley worked her way between them. As she did, she picked up male voices and then laughter. She crouched beneath the kitchen window, her head as high as she dared, constantly readjusting her position, trying to make out words and who was speaking.

It was Cal and Eddie. And they didn't sound upset.

". . . yeah, I know. Well, I wasn't gonna let her bust Carley, for Chrissake . . . Kid's been knockin' herself stupid . . . real good with Dad and Ma and the nags."

Eddie said something she couldn't make out, then ". . . but *you?*"

"Well, I told her Dad was telling me what to do and that I knew more 'n she thought I did, just from growing up around him. It was plausible."

"What'd she say?"

Cal laughed, long and mirthful, his beer laugh. "She flipped out, man. Flipped out. Didn't want me touching her horse, yadda, yadda. But she bought it. I thought she softened up a little bit before she left, too. Y'know. The nag ain't dead. Which is entirely thanks to Miss Carla-Derby-Rose, but Jewel don't know that." Carley heard the refrigerator door open and then a moment later, close again. The sound of a can opening. Then another can. "Here y'go, man."

Eddie said, "I told you not to put beer in the refrigerator. Carley. And besides, you know your mother still gets in there sometimes. Did Jewel ask if you'd seen me around? Cause y'know, I told her I've been checking the horses for her. A lot. Told you that."

"Didn't ask, didn't mention it. Neither way. Woulda told her I never saw you though, like you'd been careful-like. See what I mean?"

"Yeah, but then she might think I didn't do it."

"It's a moot point anyway."

So Cal had covered for her. Taken heat for her. Said something nice about her to Eddie. Carley squatted all the way down, her back and knees tired from the crouched position, turning over Cal's

words in her mind like ordinary old dirt—from which an unexpected vein of something precious glinted up at her. With her right
thumb, she rubbed the healing-over place on her other hand, form-
ing a broad finished line of scar tissue.

"Where the hell is she?" Eddie's voice came.

"Hiding out, I expect. Caught a glimpse of dragon lady, most
likely."

"I can't get back too late, and I damn well gotta have her with
me. I'll have to get the groceries tomorrow. Got enough to get by till
tomorrow night?"

"Dinosaurs with Dinners will be along, and they can eat that for
lunch. Just finish your beer, go out with a flashlight, and yell, 'allie,
allie in come free.'" Cal was finding himself pretty amusing.

"We also gotta develop a Plan B," Eddie said, sounding fairly
sober, unlike Cal.

"What?"

"Things could change. I mean, Jewel came right here, right into
the barn. Who knows how close she came to catching Carley? That
woulda blown the whole thing right t' the moon."

"Told you, she didn't have a clue. We're clear."

"But she's not gonna like you messin' with her horse, no matter
what you told her. I mean, I gotta think this through. Maybe I need
to, I dunno, put Carley back in rehab. Maybe Jewel will start takin'
care of the horses, and you'll just have to manage in the house."

"What about the money, man?"

"I'll give you yours as long as I can pull this off. But I gotta finesse
this, or we could both get our asses in a grinder. But y'know, if Jewel
takes her job back, even with you here, she'll know the agency money's comin' in, and I won't be able to siphon any off. I hope you've
got about enough."

"You nuts? Not even close."

It had never occurred to Carley that there was money involved.
For the second time in three minutes her thinking shifted like a
fault line in the earth, this time to reveal the disappointment of
ordinary rock, nothing better at all. She'd gotten very cold, hiding
in the bushes while night gathered around her. Now her tears made
her angry.

Carley finally showed up, freezing and bedraggled and told him and Cal that she'd hidden in the back pasture when she'd figured out that her mother was at the house. Eddie was within shouting distance of sober when she first came in but had two more beers in quick succession to celebrate her quick thinking. Smart girl! unsaddling the horse and sending him in like that. While he and Cal drank, Carley fed her grandparents dinner in front of the television and then, because Cal would be too blitzed, helped them get ready for bed, even though it was way early.

"Eddie, you're beyond buzzed. Go wash your face and gargle with toothpaste." She was talking to him like he was twelve, but he was in too good a mood to get annoyed. It took a minute to get his balance when he stood up, but then he headed for the bathroom, Cal making faces at him, which he returned. When they got out to the driveway, Carley said, "Let me drive. The last thing we need is for you to get a DUI. I'm serious. And Mom's not stupid. You'll have to tell her you've got a migraine and go right to bed. Let me do the talking."

It had been close, but they'd dodged a bullet. As Cal had pointed out, it was the second one he'd dodged, and they'd thought that was pretty funny. When Eddie repeated it to Carley on the way home, she'd said, "Yeah, that's a laugh riot," with a set to her mouth that reminded him of Jewel. So maybe he *was* a little buzzed. He'd let her drive. What else did she want?

"Hey, Carley," he leaned toward her from the passenger side. "You done good today, girl. Saved our butts. Funny how Cal said he was doin' the horses, too, huh? But you're doin' real good. I appreciate that."

"Yeah, Eddie. Save it, huh?"

"What's up your butt?" He shifted back toward the window, perplexed. They'd been getting along so fine. "You pissed 'cause I had a couple? Don't worry. Just pull in the McDonald's drive-through before we go home. I'll get me a coffee and call your mom again. I'll tell her we got something to eat in Lex because I was looking around at the truck supply place and it got late. She'll be pissed, but she'll buy it because she knows I love that place."

"Then on Saturday when you don't have the parts and can't work on the truck?"

"*Pfft.* Let me handle that. I'll get 'em on my lunch break."

"You'll go to *Lexington* on your lunch break? And when will you get the groceries for Grandma and Grandpa?"

This was beginning to feel like a police interrogation. "Back off, will you? You do your job, I'll do mine."

Carley brushed hair that had fallen from her ponytail out of her face. She looked tired and cold, and he fiddled with the heat to turn it up. She wore jeans and a long-sleeved green T-shirt, but no jacket. She'd almost forgotten to change from boots into sneakers, remembering at the last minute and running back from the truck to do it. She was real good about remembering stuff like that, he thought.

"How's the money holding out, Eddie?" Carley said, an edge to her voice. She was watching her speed carefully; he wasn't too far gone to notice that. A good driver, which surprised him. He couldn't remember when he'd last been on this side of the car with her. "I mean, they docking your pay at work or anything, taking all this time off?" she persisted when he didn't answer.

Another silence while he tried to figure out if there was anything behind the question and finally decided there couldn't be. "Nah. So far, so good. Just used a couple vacation days and sick time. I'm watching it. And you know your Mom's gettin' overtime."

"That's good. I mean, you've got a lot of extra expenses, what with Rocky and Chassie at the house now. You getting child support from Lana?"

"You joking? Hah." He warmed to his favorite subject. "That bitch couldn't hold a job if somebody put it in a bucket and tied the bucket to her wrist. She is what the politically correct like to call sanity-challenged. Not only that, the court hasn't stopped the order for me to pay child support to *her* for Rocky yet. Can you beat that? It's still comin' outta my check. Goddamn lawyers."

"So how're you managing?"

Oh shit. He'd backed himself into a bit of a corner. One beer too many, maybe. "Hey, I don't want you worrying your head about this, and don't be mentioning it to your mom. I got it covered."

"How?"

"I just do."

Headlights appeared in the distance, two narrow specks like stars fallen on the horizon. While they advanced, Eddie was silent, as if the people in the other car were intruders. Carley was taking the back way, little traveled, between farms.

"How?" she persisted when the single car passed. Was she mad? Eddie tried to get a good look at her face, but she resolutely watched the road, and he couldn't tell what her expression was. She had nothing to be mad about.

"Hey, not your concern, I'm telling you. Got some savings. Not your worry." He tried to make his tone light, not to sound like he was saying *none of your business,* which was what he meant. "Listen, don't forget about McDonald's. It's almost eight o'clock. I gotta call your mother again, and we might as well really get something to eat at the drive-through. I'll be okay by the time we get home if I eat. When we get there, you can act all mad because I dragged you up there."

"That won't be difficult," Carley said, her voice narrow and hard. Sometimes she was so much like her mother.

Jewel didn't even act annoyed. "I hope you didn't spend a fortune on that truck" was all she said. Then Eddie realized: she was relieved that *he* hadn't been here to ask where *she* had been, and he wanted to double over laughing. He was, as he'd promised Carley, sober enough to pull it off and went to bed with a "headache." She was convincing with her "I'm pissed" act and went to her room right away, too.

Eddie rinsed his mouth out with Jewel's girly blue breath stuff and then drank half the Coke he'd brought upstairs, hoping the combination would kill beer breath. He made himself wash his face and hands, thinking the smell could be there, too; Jewel claimed he stank when he had too much. The effort did him in. Getting woozy, Eddie collapsed on top of the bed in his underwear without turning out the light. When Jewel came to bed, whenever it was, she roused him as she was trying to get under the comforter.

"I hate to wake you up, but this isn't working. How about moving over and getting in?" she said. "Is your head still bad? Want me to bring you some aspirin or anything?"

"Yeah, sorry. I mean, I'll move. Gotta take a leak anyway. Already took aspirin." He hadn't. Eddie cracked his eyes, and the room swam greenish until he shut them. The room *was* light green, the comforter blue-and-green paisley. "You can go ahead and turn out the light."

He got up slowly, making his way to the bathroom while trying to stay asleep. While he stood at the toilet, Jewel called through the open door.

"Carley wouldn't answer her door. She'd just say 'leave me alone, I've gone to bed.' But her light was on. I could see it under the door. What's going on with her?"

"Dunno." True. But he came to enough to realize he didn't want her fussing or asking questions and reluctantly pushed himself to a higher degree of wakefulness. He didn't try to answer over the flushing water, but when he got into his side of the bed he said, "Honey, don't let her fool you. We get along fine these days. I told you, we went to McDonald's and all. She's just tired 'cause I puttered too long lookin' at truck stuff."

Jewel felt for his hand and squeezed it. Her hair still looked weird, but the fringe was more like regular bangs now and possible to fix so she didn't look like an alien. Eddie loved his wife and liked it when he remembered the simple beauty of just loving her right up front. Having her look more normal helped, and he clung to it lately, even in the dark, even now as he hoped he'd be able to sink back into that soft black sleep in which there were no balls to juggle, no mazes to run, no thousand-piece puzzles that might or might not be missing a crucial piece.

In the morning, he didn't have to fake the headache. It was the size of a basketball, and he could have sworn it was being used in an NBA playoff. And he really hadn't had *that* much to drink. The stress was getting to him.

After Jewel left early for work, he called in sick. Actually, he said he would try to get in by noon if he felt better. Rocky had already fed himself cereal and gotten himself off to the school bus by the time Eddie stumbled downstairs, practically blind as Hack. Unfortunately, his eyes focused enough to see Chassie leave the house dressed as if she were headed to work in a Hong Kong whorehouse rather than to class at the beauty school. How much better was he doing as a parent than his nutcase ex-wife?

On the way to the farm, he figured Carley was pissed because he was taking off another half day to get the groceries. He reached over and patted her thigh briefly. "It'll be okay," he said. "I'll put in a half day. Gotta get the groceries anyway. If you go with me, we can do it quick, and then I'll only be a couple hours late clocking in. You have no idea how much accumulated sick time I have."

She didn't yield. Wouldn't even look at him, just shook her head. "Too much to do at the house. And I gotta go get that saddle I left out."

"Okay. Y'know. I been meaning to tell you, you look good, your hair growing out to its natural color like it is. The blond is nice."

"Whatever."

"*Sheesh*, you're as bad as your mom for holding a grudge." He fell silent, figuring she was still mad about him getting buzzed.

During the day the headache abated, and the necessity of a Plan B reoccurred to Eddie. He got sweaty thinking about how things could blow up. He'd have to try to get Jewel to tell him about last night, so he could glean her intentions.

It wasn't nearly as difficult as he'd thought it was going to be. His wife was in a talkative mood that night. As she loaded the dishwasher after dinner, she suggested they take Copper for a walk.

"It's getting pretty dark," Eddie said without thinking of opportunity gained or lost, only of how tired he was. "You'd have to change clothes and all. And I'm exhausted. Long day at work." She was still in the black dress pants and pink sweater set she'd worn to the office; she'd come home and started dinner right away. Carley had gone upstairs to her room saying she wasn't hungry. Eddie knew she'd eaten at the farm with her grandparents, not that he could tell Jewel that she wasn't going hungry.

"What's up with her?" Jewel asked Eddie. Again. How should he know?

"She's okay. Told me she's just tired. She'll come down and make a sandwich when she gets hungry," Eddie said in his best reassuring voice. Carley had scarcely spoken to him on the way to or from the farm today.

"Maybe I better get over to rehab and ask around if she's doing all right," Jewel mused. "I'd have to give up a day of overtime, but she hardly says a word to me."

Eddie panicked. "Nah. No need. I went in the other day when she wasn't waiting outside. Ran into somebody who told me she was doin' great."

"Really? Was it her social worker? Her name's Annie Brooks."

"Yeah, that was the name. Lady saw me with her and just came over and said it. So how about that walk? I'll go if you want."

"Why didn't you tell me what Annie said? I mean, that's big stuff." Her eyebrows were up, but her face didn't look mad. Not yet. He needed to practically get down on his knees and be fast with the apology.

"I know. I'm sorry, just forgot. Lot goin' on at work. I forget stuff. Sorry."

"I'm just glad it's good news for once. Did she say anything else?"

"No, just that. It was real quick, on the way out, y'know. That's why I forgot. Shoulda told you."

"S'okay. How about just a short walk for some fresh air? Poor Copper, he's really been neglected lately. We're hardly ever here. If it weren't for Rocky feeding and taking him out—"

"See, it's working out," Eddie interrupted, eager to change the subject as well as put in a good word for the benefits of having his children there, although not fifteen feet away, the television set was far too loud, and Rocky, who should have been doing his homework, was watching *The Simpsons,* a show Eddie considered subversive. Chassie, as usual, was out with that boy. Controlling her was like trying to catch rain in his hands. "Son, get up to your homework," Eddie hollered over the breakfast bar into the TV din.

"It's done," Rocky called back without looking away from the screen. The back of the boy's head looked like a smaller version of Eddie's, same buzz cut, the object of merciless mocking by Chassie.

"Those grades better show it," Eddie said, an unconvincing threat Rocky ignored. "And turn that lower. It's about to break the sound barrier."

"Come on," Jewel said. "I gotta get out of here." She took Copper's leash from its hook in the closet and whistled. The beagle popped off the sofa where he'd been cuddled next to Rocky.

"Thata boy," she said, caressing Copper's ears as she hooked him up. "Rocky, thanks for taking such good care of Copper. He's lucky to have you for a buddy. Your dad and I are just going to take him on a walk with us."

"No problem," Rocky said. "He's cool. I like to do stuff with him. I'm teaching him to fetch."

"Well, I really appreciate that. He loves attention. Come on," Jewel repeated to Eddie. "Grab me my black fleece, will you? I won't change my clothes, just put on sneakers."

"I'll be in my customary class outfit," Eddie said, adjusting his balls through his jeans and winking at her. "Always dressed to go anywhere." He wore the beat-up athletic shoes he wore to work and everywhere else.

They'd only walked two houses down the road before Jewel opened up and, on her own, took Eddie right where he wanted her to go. "So, Rocky's teaching Copper to fetch," she chuckled, rolling her eyes. "I hope he gets that Copper is a *beagle*, not a Lab. Copper's idea of fetching has a lot to do with, '*Oh, look, there goes a squirrel!*'"

"I doubt he has a clue, but it's keeping them both out of trouble, so let's not burst his bubble."

"He's a good kid. Someday, when life is normal, maybe I can build some kind of real relationship with him. Teach him to ride if he wants. I went to Mom and Dad's yesterday."

Grateful, grateful for the near darkness and being dragged behind Copper with his insatiable need to sniff where every animal in the tri-state area might have peed in the past three weeks. So easy and natural not to look at his wife, not to have his breathing steady as the dog tried to dislocate his arm. "Really? You went to see your parents?"

"No. I had to see the horses for myself. Touch them, you know? I know you've been checking them for me and taking them the treats, and I don't want you to think I don't appreciate it. I hope you understand."

He wanted to play this right. Not encourage her to do it again, not unless she was going to take the whole job back, of course. Eddie waited a beat. "Well, I'm trying."

"I know. And it really makes a difference. Thank you for that."

"Thanks for what *you* said about Rocky." He waited out four or five steps of silence to stretch out the good feeling, lengthen it into what he needed to know now. "So are you thinking of starting to take care of them, like, I mean your parents? Or the horses? I mean, I thought you weren't going back there, and now you've gone twice. I mean, I sorta need to know."

"Why?" The question was curious, on the edge of sharp. Her head angled to the side, eyes narrowed. He'd gone too far.

"I just meant, if we're gettin' that income back, then, you know, not that you haven't been pulling overtime," he covered, not resisting when Copper dragged him toward the Eshbaughs' mailbox to pee on their chrysanthemums. "That yard is way too nice, don't you think? Makes ours look bad. We need to let Copper have at it." Keep it casual, he thought, mix in a bit of light humor.

She waited for the beagle to finish and for Eddie to catch up with her. "Are you asking about destroying the Eshbaughs' yard? Definitely. Or asking about the horses? Then I don't know. But that's not my point. It's that I don't know what to *think*. It's like nothing is what I thought."

"What do you mean, honey?" He knew enough to switch to the other side of her and use his free hand to reach out and take one of hers. She let him, and held on.

"Spice was in a stall."

"Wasn't when I checked on 'em. Is that bad?"

"*Cal* put him there. *Cal* took care of my horse. Well, Dad really, but Cal helped him. Been taking care of *all* the horses. He's been taking care of Mom and Dad. I talked to him."

"Did you shoot him?" He gave Jewel's hand two quick squeezes.

"That's not funny."

He leaned over as they walked and gave her an awkward kiss on the cheek. "Sorry," he whispered. "I meant it to be."

"*Any*way, *no* I didn't shoot him. I might have thought about it, but the gun wasn't right there handy, Mr. Smarty."

"Has he messed up the horses?"

"No. They all look good. Really good, to be honest, not that I'd say that to him. He said Dad found a bee sting on Spice's leg and put a cold pack on it, but it looked fine to me. His stall was clean, the cold pack was done right. All that stuff, you don't know what I'm talking about, I know. But it was all okay."

"I've been tellin' you they're all fine. Did he say he's seen me?" Eddie said, thinking she'd expect the question.

"Never mentioned it. Probably too busy laying on the couch."

"And your parents?"

"He said they're fine, the agency people are coming."

"Did you have a fight?"

"No."

"So what are you upset about?"

"I don't know. Maybe because I'm so unnecessary after all. They really don't care that I'm gone. And then today, Cal. I never would have thought he'd take care of them, let alone the horses. I don't get it. Nothing is what it seemed."

Don't step on a land mine, Eddie told himself. He just had to keep things going long enough for Cal to have the money to get himself gone. It couldn't be that much longer. "Well," he said, choosing words cautiously, "maybe sometimes things work out okay anyway?"

Hack had a moment of thinking his hearing was going. He could have sworn his wife had said, "Looks like you were right. She's not comin' back. It's a mess." He'd heard her say something was a mess plenty of times but never that he'd been right about anything.

They were lying in bed in the dark, not that darkness signaled anything to him, but he'd heard Louetta turn the light out. The soft *swoosh* of her oxygen machine was audible, so he knew it was on and the plastic tubes in her nostrils. He didn't like to notice it, but Louetta was going downhill while he was stronger and happier than he'd been in a long time.

The thing was, he reasoned, it couldn't be Jewel's absence that was making Louetta worse. Eddie had taken her to every doctor appointment. There was food in the house, that thanks to Eddie, too. Carley made sure they got a good breakfast and lunch, and they had the Meals on Wheels for dinner. Cal, in his own way, was more help than Hack had expected. He did the laundry and helped Carley

out when she gave him a list of what to do in the mornings. Eavesdropping, Hack heard how Carley kept the list short, her voice all
business. Cal *had* stopped smoking around Louetta, like the doctor
said. And he helped Louetta to the bathroom; it fell to him to clean
her up sometimes, too. More often of late.

The kicker was, Hack himself was flourishing. Carley took him
out to the barn every day now. He'd sit by the corral in Indian summer sun listening while she trained his beauties, doing what he said.
They'd brush coats and curry and clean hooves together, Carley
absorbing what he knew. Between the two of them, they'd taken
care of Spice, and he was sound as ever, no vet needed after all,
thank you very much. He hadn't lost his touch. He was still good for
something. Carley would make him go in for a nap; in some ways
she was as bad as Jewel, acting like Queen of the Barn, but it was
different. Like the old days, and he'd picked up strength from it. He
didn't want it to end.

"We're doing okay, aren't we?" he said to Louetta, not even seiz-
ing the opportunity to comment on how they'd better start praying
since he'd never been right about a thing in his life, and, if he was,
it must mean the End of Days and Second Coming was about two
minutes away. Hack didn't believe in that crap, but Louetta did, so
he'd just have been saying it to annoy her. And he didn't want to
annoy her now. He wanted her to say *yes*.

"Hack, I'm thinking maybe I should call Jewel. Maybe I should
tell her I'm sorry. I kept thinking she'd come around, y'know."

Hack felt his way through the rumpled sheet between them on
the double bed—Cal hadn't straightened up or made their bed this
morning, though Carley had told him to—and found Louetta's arm,
then her hand. He was buying time to think. He'd heard some of
the goings-on a couple of nights earlier when Cal and Eddie had
both gotten drunk and Carley had fixed their Meals on Wheels
and helped them to bed early. His hearing was a lot sharper than
Louetta's, who'd been paying attention to the television anyway. But
he'd picked up this much: Jewel *had* come, evidently while he and
Louetta were both napping, when Carley took Red out on the trail.
He'd gleaned that Jewel didn't have a clue that Carley was here. And
would shit a whole house worth of bricks if she knew.

"Notice how much more Cal is doing, though?" Hack said. "I mean, I think this is doing him good. If you call Jewel and ask her to come back, you'll have to make Cal go." It was a calculated gamble. He couldn't believe she'd put herself in reverse. Old cars have rusty gears. Beside, how would Louetta feel if she heard Jewel had come to see the horses and not even checked in on her own parents? No, it was best to keep his peace.

Hack worried something really *was* wrong with Louetta when he defended Cal and she didn't immediately challenge his motive. She didn't even realize that they'd switched positions. It wasn't that Hack didn't miss Jewel or didn't want her back. He did, for sure. Cal was no replacement. But he didn't want to lose what he had now, being out with the horses every day. And just between him and Carley, he'd started her quietly looking for a two year old he could buy. His granddaughter could become a fine trainer with him out there working with her.

Hack squeezed Louetta's hand. "You doin' okay? Feelin' decent, I mean?"

"Breathin's tight. I guess I just called it wrong with Jewel. Don't recognize myself anymore. Used to care—you know how Jewel kept this place. Clean, spit polish. Carley's doin' fine with the meals, but the house is dirty. I guess that's Cal's job, the way they got it set up, but, thing is, I'd a thought that would make me crazy. Dirty floors, dirty dishes, junk left around. I don't much care. Now why's that? Just called it wrong with Jewel. Called a lot of things wrong, maybe."

There had been a time when Hack would have crowed, done a victory dance, and considered his entire life worthwhile to have heard those words from his wife. Now he didn't want to hear them at all.

"It'll work out," he said. "Just like you said at the beginning, it'll work out in time. I was the one wrong."

Louetta didn't say any more, but Hack took comfort in her silence. He lay awake a long time after she'd gone to sleep, his hand folded lightly over hers, listening to the whir of her oxygen, which, if his hearing hadn't been so acute, would have drowned out the crickets. He wished he'd thought to ask Carley exactly what phase the moon was in; he liked to know if the room had the silvery sheen it did when it was full or nearly so. He tried to settle himself by remembering: how the horses looked in starry pasture, the night music of the insects and plashes of pond life, the enormity of the harvest moon that had risen the night he'd named the new foal Moonglow. This was the most disconcerting conversation he'd had with his wife in years, to say nothing of the most intimate. She hadn't pulled her hand away as they spoke nor did he move his now but kept hers in his like something found.

<hr />

In bed tonight, I am edgy as the squirrels that are Copper's nemeses, their wary eyes darting side to side as they anticipate his release from the back door and beat his arrival at the birdfeeder they are raiding by a timely leap onto the lowest maple branch.

"Maybe you're thinking about going back, the Eldercare job I mean? Sounds like it sorta worked out okay, talking to Cal. Didn't it, sweetheart?" Eddie says, rubbing my arm, then my shoulder, and sneaking his way down to my breast. This after he said he was *so* exhausted when I wanted to take Copper for a walk. There's almost a pleading tone in his voice, but I can't tell whether he's hoping I'll try to get my job back or I'll make love with him, something he's never too tired for.

"You don't understand. I can't . . ."

"Why?"

I lie in the dark trying to find words. In the end it's easier to make love, because what can I tell him? *I* don't understand. And what does Eddie care about understanding? *Being* is enough for him, an utterly concrete, tactile being in the world while I want inside and outside to match, words and feeling, appearance and reality. And none of it does right now, which has me, as I said, edgy as the squirrels. So I take refuge in Eddie's world, trying to disappear for a night into a sheer physical experience that might blot out *why, if, how, maybe*, all those, until I can find sleep.

"Wow," he says afterward. "Who unleashed you, tiger?"

"Let me sleep," I murmur, trying to go under. "I don't want to talk."

"Who are you, and what have you done with my wife?" he says, propped on an elbow, the way I usually am, while my back is turned, the way his usually is.

I've tried to just breathe for a few days, live as if anxiety weren't a mouse eating holes in the drywall of my mind. Deflecting Eddie's questions about what I intend to do, telling him "nothing" for the time being, I go to the office, put in overtime while it's available, pick up Rocky at football practice while Eddie takes Carley to and from rehab. She seems remote as the stars and spends the evenings in her room. Eddie says she's okay, it's just that Rocky and Chassie get on her nerves downstairs with their bickering. Every night I want to spend time with her, but when I knock on her door, she says she's tired and doesn't want to talk. I worry that Roland's on her mind. He's still in jail. I check the Internet every day at work to make sure, my guilty pleasure. If Carley knew, she'd hate me for it, but it was the right thing to do. She must think he's moved on. I hope she hates *him* for it. Rehab is working, because she's sober and looking more and more healthy. Why do I feel as if I've lost her?

Mama and Daddy are obviously doing all right with the agency, which I should be glad about, but instead it is painful proud flesh on me, like something the vet will have to debride and excise.

I have to go back. I tell myself it's the horses, that I need to reassure myself that Spice is really all right. And that's almost as true as it is that I just long to put my arms around his neck, love and talk to each horse in turn, and relax into the comfort of their acceptance. Maybe I can find a way to ride, just get up bareback this time, while I see how it goes. But maybe there's a way to just *see* Mama and Daddy, too, away from Cal. This is the longest we've ever been apart. I think about it, and then my angry side sparks. No, dammit. I took care of them. They should have cared about me.

Twice I start to tell Eddie I'm going to go over again, but both times I let the moment pass. I could go on Saturday, but instead I put in for a half day of vacation on Friday afternoon. I'll make sure my work is done so no one has to cover something that's mine to do.

The sun is at one-thirty on a brilliant blue October day when I leave the office, a bit later than I'd hoped. I worked through lunch, finished payroll, and changed in the bathroom. The air is clean as washed sheets, and the uneasiness I've not shaken dissipates a bit in the glory of the day. *Stop being such a worrywart,* I tell myself. Mrs.

Bladen, my fourth-grade teacher, told me that once, not that I knew what a worrywart was, and she didn't explain it.

I get all the way to our road before I decide not to hide the car but not to pull in the driveway, either. A compromise: I'll just park farther on down the road and walk back, then up the driveway to the barn. That way the car won't make noise and invite attention. If this works and Cal leaves me alone, maybe I can go back to taking care of the horses. Really, they all should start supplemental hay now. The grass is dying. Daddy can't see to know the condition of the pasture, and Cal doesn't know about these things, no matter what he says.

I park and for no reason check myself in the rearview mirror. Big-eyed and pale. My bangs are down to my eyebrows now, and the sides, sort of hang like they don't know what else to do. But it's better than it was. I take a rubber band out of the ashtray and pull the back into a ponytail and bobby pin the sides. Breathe deep. Breathe again. And again.

Scarcely past the mailbox, my sneakers start onto the weedy gravel at the end of the driveway, a sound like they're eating cold cereal, and I'm watching the back door warily, feeling guilty and scared and defiant all at once. What I'm on the lookout for is Cal. What I see, though, as I come up the small rise in the land is movement in the paddock behind the barn. I quicken my pace to get where I can see beyond the fence. Spice is in a slow jog on a lunge line. Cal? He knows how to lunge a horse? Cal's hair isn't that long, and he wouldn't be in that bright-red shirt that confuses me with its familiarity.

"Carley!" My voice is a frog-croak of shock and anger, and she doesn't hear me the first time.

I don't know how she misses my approach except that she is so focused on Spice, her eyes on him as intently as if she were deciphering a code. "Carley!"

She startles out of her concentration, jerking on the line, and then, seeing me, is frightened. "Whoa, whoa, boy," she calls to Spice, who reacts to her by breaking gait and bucking once. "Whoa, off that front leg. Settle down, atta boy." Spice trots a few more steps, then walks. "Whoa, good boy, steady," Carley repeats.

"What the hell is going on here?" I climb the fence and head into the corral toward her, intending to take the line away from her.

"Let me handle it, Mom. Just let me alone. I know what I'm doing."

"You're supposed to be at rehab. Why are you *here*? I'm taking you back right now." I head right at her, holding out my hand for the line.

Carley slides it behind her back. "I'm taking care of Spice. When's the last time *you* took care of him?"

"This isn't your concern. How'd you get here?"

"What do you mean it's not my concern? Stay back!" She raises her voice but not enough to bother Spice, I notice. She reels him partway toward her, then, walking to meet him, caresses his head and neck before using the line as a lead rope to walk him in big slow circles around the paddock. She gets around the paddock six or seven times.

While she does, I cool myself down enough to realize what's happened.

"Carley," I say, as evenly as possible. "Roland got out, didn't he? He brought you here so you and he could score with Cal. Where is he?"

She opens the gate from the paddock into the front pasture, removes my horse's halter, and turns him out. I let her, though my heart had been set on working him myself. I'm not prepared for the rage on her face when she turns around.

"You fucking think you know everything. You know nothing. *Nothing*." Little drops of spit fly off one of the words and arc into the sunlight.

"I know that you need to be back in rehab. They'll help. We'll talk to Annie." I'm pedaling my voice down to soft, calm, slow, even kind. Maybe she's high. I don't want to make the kind of mistakes I've made before with verbal fireworks, no matter that I'm calculating how to get a restraining order against Roland, and furious I didn't check the goddamn Internet before I left work today. Who posted bail? His family are all deadbeats.

"Oh my God. You're the one who's reality-impaired. You want to blame Roland? When you went behind my back and put him in jail? Who do you think's been taking care of things here while you've been doing your little sit down strike? Talk about drugging yourself." Her arms fly up. "Uh-uh, you're not the only one who can go behind peoples' backs, Ma. Maybe you better talk to your precious Eddie and his new best friend, Cal. Find out from Eddie how I get here every day. Find out how the Eldercare agency thinks *you're* still working here."

I stand stunned in the middle of the corral. Her torrent runs on over me while I drown, disbelieving.

Cal's voice penetrates the noise in my head. "Carley! Carley!" The back storm door bangs against the house. "Oh shit. Jewel! You here? You better get inside. I called the ambulance. Ma's . . . I think she might be dead."

In Beauty School

EDDIE KNEW SOMETHING WAS off almost as soon as his truck raised the dust in his in-laws' driveway. For one thing, the barn doors were closed, and none of the horses were in sight; normally at least one was in the corral, and Carley was still messing with it even though she knew damn well he'd be in a hurry. Now the place almost looked shuttered, like its eyes were closed, and it gave him the creeps. He put the truck in park and went in the back door without calling out his presence.

It didn't matter. As soon as he was in the kitchen he knew they'd been busted. Someone had scrubbed the room down like it hadn't been since . . . oh shit. How the hell had he missed her car? Jewel must have parked on down the road, past the mailbox, to hide it. Eddie stood at the open door, his hand still on it, as the meaning of the moment grew in his mind. She would never understand, never.

The sound of the vacuum cleaner started up, coming from the living room. He could probably make it out of there undetected. Too late. Carley rounded the corner and came into the kitchen.

"Eddie! I tried to call you. Why didn't you answer your cell? Oh my god, Grandma, she's . . . Grandma's dead. Mom's here. She's in the other room."

"Louetta? What? Louetta's not dead."

Carley started crying, something he could see wasn't new. Her face already looked all bleary and red. But his first thought was that she must be wrong. It wasn't like Louetta had been in critical condition or anything. He took her hand and led her out the kitchen door, down the two steps and to the side, so they'd be out of sight. "No. I don't get it. She can't be. You called your mother? What?" He was stammering, trying to focus himself, but, more, trying to get Carley to focus. It was already twilight, and a full moon, the harvest moon, was rising just above the trees, the very tops of which were like the embers of a dying fire from the last bit of sunset. Venus was large and surreal-looking.

The girl shook her head as if she couldn't find words and wiped her cheek with the back of her hand. She was still in barn clothes, he noticed, a red flannel shirt, dirty jeans, and boots. Her hair was pinned up, as she had it when she was working the horses. "Not me. She was already here. Cal found her."

"Cal found your mother?" Eddie was completely confused. Could she be talking like this from being high? "Where's Cal now?"

"He's got Grandpa." A fresh waterfall.

"Carley, for God's sake. *Where?*"

"In the tack room, I think. Cal said I should wait for you and then come out and get a horse for Grandpa. Grandpa says he's got to be on a horse. Mom wouldn't get Moonie for him, and he started to feel his way out of the house, so Cal walked him. Mom's in this, like, cleaning frenzy."

Eddie's head felt like a mass of cobwebs, distracted by the reference to getting "Moonie," which sounded like the religious cult thing. He set that aside, deciding it wasn't important right then. "Where is Louetta? Grandma?" he persisted, speaking slowly as if she were impaired.

She answered the same way, as if *he* were. "They took her away. They took her body. Away. The ambulance people, two men and a woman. They said she was already gone, and they took her away. But, Eddie, Mom has flipped out."

"What do ya mean? 'Cause she's cleaning?"

"Like, she slams the vacuum cleaner into the couch and says, '*You can't know anything. Nothing is true, everything's a lie, nothing's what you think.*'" Carley pantomimed the wand hitting furniture with each phrase, rage or despair or both. "And she's back and forth, crying and then she's not crying but with a bad look, like that night. You know. The gun." Carley looked down at her scarred hand, then back up at Eddie.

"No. No, she wouldn't. Not again," he said uncertainly and touched her shoulder before letting his hand drop awkwardly back to his side. "You're sure about this?" But the thought that Carley might have used something had passed, and the question was rhetorical. "Should I go in?" he said, hoping she'd say, *No, you'd better leave.*

"Yeah. Yeah, see if you can get through to her. I don't know what to do. We can't leave her like this."

It was strange to him, hearing the *we*. Gratifying, the loneliness of the moment alleviated enough that he touched her shoulder again and met her eyes when he nodded. "Here," he said, handing her his cell phone, which was, indeed, turned off. He'd been careless. "Call Chassie, will you? Tell her what's going on, and have her find Rocky. God knows where he is. Jewel was supposed to pick him up. I'll go in by myself."

"Okay," and she took it in her hand. Then Carley shocked him by putting her arms around him and her head against his chest. Impulsively, he wrapped his arms around her, cheek on the top of her head.

"It'll be all right," he whispered, even though he doubted it. And he kissed the top of her head, as he would have Chassie, when he felt deep heaving through her. His own eyes were wet, some for Louetta and some for the collapse of his hope. Eddie rubbed Carley's back, and when they each let go, his shirt was damp from her face.

He tried not to startle her. "Jewel? Honey, it's me," he said, approaching from the side. Just as Carley had said, she was vacuuming, in the living room now, as if it were Judgment Day and Jesus were about to knock on the front door to do a sanitation inspection. "Damn, honey, hold up," he said as she turned, brandishing the wand like a saber.

"Who are you?"

"Jewel, you're scaring me. You know me."

"I don't know anybody anymore. I know who I *thought* you were. Get out of here. My mother is dead."

"I know. I'm sorry. I'm so sorry, honey." He put his hand out, reaching toward her.

Jewel, who had been waving the vacuum wand above her head, slammed it down. "Get away!"

A sear of pain. Eddie jerked his hand back with a loud exclamation. "God . . . ah—"

"Get away from me. I mean it," she said, her voice a needle scratching over the words.

Eddie doubled over his wrist, putting it in the fold of his body, sheltering it with his other arm. Light-headed, eyes watering, he put one knee to the ground to steady himself.

"My God, Jewel," he whispered, looking up, crying. "What next? You gonna cut the rest of your hair off? Or, wait, the gun is around here somewhere, isn't it? You can go ahead and shoot me."

"I don't know you," she said. Her voice had gone flat, but her eyes still had a dangerous look.

Still on one knee, cradling his arm, his voice went scratchy with pain. "Look, I'm sorry. I guess I did everything wrong. At least I tried. I didn't shave my head or just quit like you. Just like you tried with Carley, I was trying for my kids. And for you. I tried to save things."

"You *used* Carley, you took her out of rehab. You lied about *everything*. For *money*." A hissed accusation. "You knew my mother was dying, and you didn't tell me."

"I didn't know Lou was worse, I swear. Took her to every appointment. Got all her medicine. But, yeah, I did ask Carley for help." Eddie looked down, ashamed for a moment. Then, "But I wouldn't give her the car. I told Cal I'd kill him myself if she got near any booze or drugs or he put himself anywhere near her. She's doin' *good*. Sober. Healthy-looking. She loves the horses, and she took over, and she's done *right*. We kept the place goin', Jewel. Your mom, she kept firing everyone anyway. You know how she is. Was." His wrist was throbbing. He looked back down at the bruise that was rising, reddish-purple like a plum.

"I don't know you," she started again.

He felt ridiculous then, looking up at her, and used the arm of Hack's chair to hoist himself to a stand as he interrupted. "Look at yourself, Jewel. Do you look like yourself, for God's sake? We're all strangers here."

Jewel's face contorted into either a dry sob or rage. Eddie thought she was going to dissolve, fall over in grief, but he didn't have the balls to try to put his arms around her. She was still holding the vacuum cleaner wand, and he was supporting his injured wrist with the other hand.

"Cal said she was by that window when she died," Jewel said, pointing. Her eyes were glassy. "That's where he found her. She must have seen me. I walked right up the driveway. He thought she might have been trying to open the window. Oh my God, was she trying to call me?"

Eddie stepped forward and wrapped his good arm around his wife. She didn't strike back, but her body didn't yield either.

The churchy part of Louetta's funeral was about mercy, and mercifully short as if to demonstrate that concept. As far as Carley was concerned, it was the rest of it that was hell, first getting her mother there and then the nightmare burial that was like an early Halloween show.

She asked Chassie to help her get Jewel dressed, and her mother tolerated their putting makeup on her so she wouldn't look so dead herself. Jewel was going to leave her hair in a ponytail, but Chassie said, "No, let me," and did it with a curling iron after she shaped it with scissors. Carley said it was amazing how Chassie got it to blend so pretty, not look hacked up anymore. She said it for her mother's benefit, but she didn't mind that Chassie took it in.

"Thanks. We learn this stuff in beauty school," Chassie said, looking pleased. "We're supposed to call it cosmetology, but I think it's nicer to call it what people really want. You know? Everyone wants their most beautiful selves, don't you think?"

Carley nodded. "Good point."

"If you want, I can soften up that stripe in your hair real quick. I've got stuff right in my room, from highlighting mine. Just take a couple minutes, then you wait twenty minutes and wash it. I mean, only if you want."

Carley looked in the mirror and thought, *Grandma said my hair is so butt-ugly, the horses think I'm a zebra.* "Yeah. If you've got time. Thanks."

Meanwhile, Jewel just sat there in her own bedroom, stiff and silent as a mannequin, the blue drapes drawn as if to shut out hope. Carley and Chassie hadn't had to clean the house, fortunately, because everyone was going to Carley's Grandpa's after the funeral instead of back here. It was better for him, people said, to be in his own environment. *People* included Chassie, Rocky, Eddie, her mom's coworkers, and Eddie's coworkers, not that it was any of their business. Eddie's ex, Crazy Lana, wanted to come, too, but Eddie said, "No way, José," and Chassie agreed. "She just thinks there'll be good cake," she said, rolling her eyes.

Carley had been relieved to have Chassie giving her a hand during the funeral preparations with the Assorted Fruits and Nuts that were their tangled family. They'd been trading eye rolls. She'd gone so far as to ask Chassie to help her look for Nadine. Eddie had tried to call for Hack's sake, but Nadine's phone was disconnected. Eddie was so pissed he just said, "Screw it," and didn't do another thing. Cal shrugged his agreement with Eddie and was no help. Even though Jewel was zoned-out, Carley knew Eddie, to say nothing of her mother, would jump off the nearest cliff to the *drugs* conclusion if they knew she was going to Nadine's. That was pure crap; Carley just thought that Nadine ought to be given a chance to be at her own mother's funeral even if the two had parted on pretty bad terms.

Carley couldn't think of a way to ask Chassie to keep her company—maybe it was asking for protection, but that didn't sound right—except by confiding in her.

"Let's do it," Chassie said, as casually as if she were giving Carley a piece of gum.

They lied about where they were going ("shopping"), drove to Nadine's last address in the Woodhill section of Lexington, and asked around enough to find that Nadine had given the landlord and other people the slip six weeks earlier. Carley, who'd once been comfortable there, known people, was eyed warily. She'd tried to avoid being recognized.

"Think they're covering for her?" Chassie asked when they were back in her car.

"I know what you're saying. People around here are sketchy. But more likely, Nadine really does owe them a bunch of money. They seemed more mad than anything."

"What happens now? I mean, how do we find her?"

"We don't. Families do lose people. Sometimes they show up again. Shit, look at Cal. Seven years . . . and then y'gotta watch out for what trouble they're packing if they do."

"Well, you're not sketchy," Chassie said, grinning for a moment and slugging Carley's thigh.

Carley wondered if Chassie really hadn't sensed the restless danger that had been a scratch below the surface. No point in freaking her out now. And did Chassie really not know perfectly well just how sketchy Carley was? No way Eddie hadn't told her about Roland, and Carley's gig in rehab. Good grief, *Chassie* wasn't the blind one. She'd seen the great bandaged hand and could see the scar right now; Carley's hand was in plain view, resting on the thigh Chassie had just slugged. No, she knew about her and Cal, the whole barn scene. Did she just not *get* any of what went on around her? When Carley stuffed her hair under Jewel's gardening hat and let the wide pale brim flop low before they got out of the car to ask about Nadine, all Chassie said was, "I love that hat." What was it with this girl?

Chassie pointed ahead. "Wanna stop at that grease factory and get a Coke?" She was inviting Carley into her clear-skinned, short-skirted, simple, leftover high school trashy prettiness, a world with girlfriends and vapid music and even more vapid boyfriends. Carley didn't want that world, but she'd also never been invited in. And look what Chassie had done today. Given her a compliment, too.

Thanks, really thanks, had risen from Carley's chest to her throat, but tears wouldn't fit Chassie's grin, and they'd both be embarrassed, so she said, "Only if that Coke comes with fries and a burger. You drove. I'll pay. Your dad gave me money to get groceries yesterday and said I could keep the change. I've got almost fifteen bucks."

"You're on," Chassie said.

So, no Nadine, but at least they were pulling off something, however pathetic. The day her grandma died, when Eddie went in to deal with her mother, Carley had thought there was no hope. She'd thought that if there was a funeral at all, there would need to be a metal detector to make sure the mourners were disarmed. Her mother scared her, unapproachable, hand scrubbing the most remote corners and every one of her grandma's angel collection. The frightening part was that even when Jewel was holding a sponge, her eyes made Carley think the sponge was loaded with bullets instead of soap. When Eddie arrived, she'd been mowing the decrepit shag carpet with the vacuum.

Carley had gone on to the tack room after she and Eddie first talked. Her grandpa was there, out of the house where his wife had died, sitting on one of the two old folding chairs, looking spent and frail as a pile of twigs. He was crying, and Cal had pulled his chair next to Grandpa so he could hold his hand. She hadn't thought Cal could do that. "Get me my beauties," Grandpa sobbed, only Cal couldn't understand what he said.

"He says he wants his beauties. The horses," Carley translated when Cal looked to her. Cal was crying himself, only with his eyes, not his voice. Carley scanned the room but didn't see even a beer can, and that wasn't like Cal, especially with bad stuff going down.

"What do you think? Okay to get them in again?" Cal said.

"I came out to do that. You told me before," she reminded him, although she shifted her weight and rubbed her arms, angling for time while she thought about it, not sure this was really the best idea. Was he going to be content with just touching them? It was getting cold, and Hack only wore one of his old cotton Western shirts, long-sleeved, the plaid faded to the color of river stones.

But she lifted halters off their hooks and threaded them over her arm, scooped out a bucket of grain. "Be back soon," she said and went out to cut through the paddock. She called the horses in the same way her mother always had, standing just behind the fence and banging on the bucket. She'd get them in and tied and then run in for a jacket for her grandfather rather than try to explain to her mother how she'd let him get sick and die just now.

Almost as soon as Carley got her name out, Moonbeam appeared, Charyzma a nose ahead of her, the others a length behind. Carley let Moonie stick her muzzle in the grain bucket first, then put the halter on her and let her through the two gates, into and through the corral, and did a quick tie while she opened one side of the barn doors. Then she brought her inside and tied her in the center aisle. Her grandfather would be sheltered, and maybe he wouldn't ask her to ride with him. There's a skill to ponying another horse and rider, and she and her grandfather had planned to start practicing in the corral this week. She wanted to learn for his sake, but she sure as hell didn't want to start when he was this shaky. She was pretty distracted herself.

But then Eddie led her mother out to the barn by the hand. His other arm was bent at the elbow, tucked along his belt. "Here, honey. Here's something good. Carley's got one of the horses in for your dad." He was talking to Jewel as if she'd gone mad but was still within calling distance of normal. "Hey, Carley, what d'ya say, could you get your mom's horse in, too? I mean, so she can just see him? Would you mind?"

She picked up his tone. "No, that's cool. Here, Mom. Hold out your arm for these other halters and lead ropes. I don't know why I grabbed them all at once anyway. I'll only take Spice's with me this time."

Jewel stuck her right arm out to receive the other tack. She didn't say a thing.

Spice and the other horses were grazing just on the other side of the corral fence, expectant. "Just you, boy, right now, just you," Carley said, sliding on his halter.

When she brought Spice into the barn, Jewel was standing by Moonie with her face next to his and her hand on his neck. When she saw Spice, she crossed the few steps and hugged his neck.

"See? The beauties are still fine. See what a good job Carley's done, honey? Ask her about his leg. Honest to God, we were all just trying to take care of them. And everyone," Eddie said, too perky in the human silence. His tone and voice seemed to keep going after he stopped, mixing all wrong into Hack's crying on Moonie's mane and the small sounds of the horses' shifting hooves and swishing tails. The wide barn door was open and the noise of crickets came there, too, arguing the earth's irresolvable and wordless losses.

Carley said, "I'll go get brushes and picks." She spoke softly but enough to dispel Eddie's echo. She worried she was missing something and the barn might ignite at any minute, fiery, deadly roof timbers falling to crush them all. Going to the tack room twice— she'd go back for hoof oil—would give her a chance to unload the barn gun, put the bullets in her pocket.

Her mother and grandfather fiddled with Spice and Moonbeam first, giving them each a long, thorough grooming. Carley had already taken care of them earlier in the day, but they got curried

and brushed all over and their feet cleaned again. Then they were
stalled while the other two were brought in for the same treatment.
Full darkness came with a light, imperceptible step. Cal ordered two
pizzas, and Eddie gave Carley his wallet to pay for it. Jewel wouldn't
eat any, but she made her father have some.

"I gotta call Chassie again and make sure she's there for Rocky.
Your mom may not be willing to come home with me," Eddie whispered to Carley when they went to the house to get napkins and
soda. "If not, I'm stayin' here with her. I won't leave her with Cal.
Too many bad memories. I can sleep downstairs on your old bed."
They stood outside the barn conferring a moment. Eddie carried
two more jackets he'd rummaged out of the closet. God only knew
whose they'd been in some other life. Something was wrong with
one of his arms. He looked like he was trying not to use it.

"What's the matter?" Carley pointed at Eddie's left arm but didn't
touch it, in case she was right.

"Ran into a door. 'S all right."

"I'll go stay with Rocky if Chassie already has plans," Carley said.

"You'd do that?"

"You'd have to let me take your truck to get there."

"Yeah, sure. Thanks, Carley. I appreciate that."

Embarrassed, Carley looked away because Eddie was swiping his
face with the back of his hand. The sounds of the autumn night were
locust chirps and buzzes and frog songs, and his sniffle sounded
like one of them. The yard lights illuminated them from one side
but didn't show red eyes, swollen features.

"It's been a bad day," he said. "I'm real sorry about your grandma.
I don't think we did anything wrong. With her, I mean."

"God, Eddie," she answered, though the thought had already
occurred to her. "Do you think we might've? I mean, *should've* done
something?"

"We took her to every appointment. She was on oxygen already. I
think her body just got tired. That's what I think. We all did the best
we could." He gave his shrug.

"Do ya think Mom's blaming us?"

"More herself, sounds like t' me. Feels so bad she never saw her,
y'know."

"Guilt on steroids."

"I got me some of that, too. But it wasn't like the agency people worked out. Not saying I didn't benefit, though. That's the rub."

Carley waited until he met her eyes. "Eddie, I'm not using, not one bit, if that's what she's thinking."

"I know that, honey. And whatever she thinks right now, you've done a good thing. *I'm* telling you. You've done a real good job. I'm proud of you."

Carley imagined he thought her fresh tears were over her mother, adrift in a sea of guilt and grief and rage, or for her grandmother, bossy and difficult as she might have been sometimes.

"Thanks," she said. "Thanks."

The burial seemed to be a turning point for her mother, though Carley had no idea what might have made it so because she herself found it so pathetic, everyone in cobbled-together mourning outfits, except Chassie, who had a low-cut, thigh-skimming black number. Carley stood next to Chassie by choice. Her mother was between Eddie and her grandfather anyway. And next to her Grandpa was Cal in a sports coat that belonged to Eddie, an iffy fit since the sleeves were too long, and it was too big in the chest and back. The pants were Hack's and matched the coat okay but were high-water, and Cal wore sneakers because nobody thought about shoes until the last minute when it *was* the last minute and plain too late. Dark socks, probably her grandpa's. At least Cal had washed his hair and shaved. Carley whispered to Chassie that it was probably the first time he'd showered since he'd shown up.

Everybody stood around this big depressing hole in the ground that was covered with Astroturf to make it look like something else. It was neon-obvious, though, because a short distance away was another oblong hole that wasn't covered, which Carley thought was in very bad taste, no matter how pressed the mortuary people were for time. And to make matters worse, Louetta's cousin's daughter, Delia, brought her kids, who ran around the cemetery during the service as if it were a playground. Carley found it plain embarrassing to be even distantly related to Delia, but it had to be worse for her mother, so she and the rest of the family did what they could to smooth over the fiasco the kids created. It was weird how she didn't mind Eddie telling her what to do and actually ended up admiring how Eddie took charge.

After the burial, the fog around her mother seemed to clear, as if she'd shaken her head. (Well, that made it sound more dramatic than it was, Carley said to herself, but both she and Eddie had noticed, eyeing each other in the way of allies.) When the minister said the last amen, Jewel let Cal take their father's arm, and they led him toward the parked cars. Carley walked five or six steps behind, with Eddie, Chassie, and Rocky, afraid to approach.

Halfway to where the cars were parked, Jewel stopped and turned. "Where are you all?" she said, motioning them forward with a hand that held a crumpled tissue. She wiped her eyes, then stuffed the tissue in the purse that dangled from her elbow. "Come on, we've got people to feed," she said, straightening her shoulders. She waited for them all to catch up, and they walked on, abreast. Carley overheard her mother speak quietly to Eddie, who was beside her now. "I'm sorry I hurt your arm," she said.

"Shh," he said. "It's fine."

And even that wasn't the end of things to shock her that day.

Before they made it to the parking lot, Cal stepped out of the line and blocked Jewel's way. The lockstep stopped its forward progression. Carley, immediately frantic, looked at Eddie. But instead of slugging Cal in the gut, Jewel just said, "What is it?"

Cal cleared his throat and said, "I need a minute. In private."

Immediately, Eddie jumped the line and faced Cal, making himself into a wall in front of Jewel. "You'll be leaving Jewel alone now, Cal, is what you'll be doing."

Carley started to join Eddie, but Chassie pulled her back, held her hip to hip, and stuck her lips practically inside Carley's ear. "If they fight, you'll be in Dad's way. He can take Cal." Carley knew something was wrong with Eddie's left arm, which was covered by his shirt and jacket, but she yielded into the immeasurable silence. Time was sucked out of the world, and there was only stillness, sky, the white sun, fear.

Then Carley knew something was different, because Jewel stepped up and said, "It's okay," softly to Eddie, and that she'd meet them all at the cars. Carley was no less afraid. Chassie put her arm around Carley's waist and waited with her.

"Jewel," Cal started, but then his tongue stalled. He hadn't planned this out at all, and now he felt he'd picked the wrong time, wrong place. Stupid, standing out here. The family probably was walking backward to the parking lot with binoculars trained on him. But he'd put it off since their mother died, not knowing if he'd do more harm. When he told her about Ma being at the window when she died, it had flipped Jewel out bad.

"Just want to say I, um, I didn't mean to make a mess of things. And I'm real sorry about Carley . . . before." He blinked in the brilliance of the daylight. "For what it's worth, when Eddie was bringin' her t' the house, everything was straight up. I didn't want you thinkin' I . . . and she never used nothin'. She was real good to Ma and Dad—"

"Dad told me," she interrupted, and when she looked at him there wasn't loathing on her face, which surprised him. Jewel looked like somebody had fixed her up pretty good. Her hair was done nice, that chain-saw job hidden with curls around her face, and she had makeup on, but her eyes were tired-out in the center of it. The sunlight aiming itself on her face didn't leave anything concealed. The lack of active hatred bolstered him to keep going.

"Just want to say I'm sorry. Know that don't make it right."

There were beats of silence, and Cal almost didn't go on. Eddie hadn't known if it would make things better or worse. Jewel had pretty well gone insane when Ma died, and now that the burial was over, and she had suddenly talked to them all, maybe it was best to leave things alone.

"We'd better get going. Everyone will get back to the house before us," Jewel said.

On the other hand, even though she hadn't responded to his apology, she hadn't shot him, either. And the contents of Cal's pocket—it had to be that—made him feel as if his chest were igniting, if regret and sadness and loss could burn flesh. Or even love, wordless and far too late.

"Wait. Ma, well, I dunno if she was gonna ask Carley to give this to you or maybe ask Eddie. Well, that's not the point, but this was in Ma and Dad's room. It was with her stuff, y'know, by her side of the bed. Anyway, I'm tryin' to say I saw it and I took it. Don't know if it's better or worse for you, but I gotta give it to you."

"What is it, Cal?" she said.

This was strange. He couldn't decipher if that was a neutral resignation in her voice or something hiding three feet back from the edge of kindness. He'd only had one good shot of Jim Beam to stiffen him for his mother's funeral, nothing to make him hear things funny. He needed to replay it over and over to sort it out, but there wasn't time.

He pulled a folded sheet of paper from the inside pocket of his borrowed sports coat and gave it to her. As Jewel took it, Cal touched her shoulder, wishing he dared more, but only turned and walked toward the cars. He put the hand that had touched his sister into his pocket, risking one quick glance over his shoulder to see what she was doing.

Dear Jewel,

Your Daddy said I chose Cal over you from the beginning and this time I drove you out forever. I thought you'd come back and I could have both you and Cal, but turns out your Daddy was right. Maybe nothing wrong with what I wanted, but wrong how I went about it. So I told him I'd call you and say I was sorry, but then he said, well, give it more time. He said Cal's doing better, and Carley keeps things going, and maybe it will all work out on its own after all. But then I thought on it and maybe what your Daddy likes is that Carley has him out in the barn every day now. He lives for his beauties, as you know. I guess everyone does, sort of. Thing is, I messed up on seeing mine. I don't know who's right and who's wrong, so I decided to write and you decide.

I'm not right these days, Jewel. My chest hurts and my heart jumps around and it's hard to breathe. They take me to the doctor, don't think they don't. But now I'm scared I won't see you again

if I don't ask you to come back. I don't mean to come do any
work. It's just I miss you. I used to say none of the aides did
anything right, and you did do it best, but it would have been
better if I just said I love you. I'm sorry I didn't say that before so
I'm saying it now. And that you're a real good daughter.
  I'd like to tell you what I learned in my life. It's a real short
list (Ha Ha). If you don't come back, then just remember don't
be blind even though you do come by it honest. (Ha Ha again). I
got stuck on one way of seeing things. I forgot to try to be better,
and I'm sorry.

Love,
Mama

"Lotsa ways to be blind," my father likes to say.

I was right when I said that nothing was what it seemed. I was wrong when I thought I knew what it really was instead. At least partly. I saw the surface well enough but not the layers beneath with all their colors and texture. The problem is that you never know when you're actually seeing the whole picture, all the way out to the sides and bottom, all the layers. Maybe the truth has to put together what everybody sees.

It's been four months since Mama died. Life has rearranged itself into a Plan B I never foresaw. Carley got certified by the County Eldercare agency and lives with Dad, taking care of him and the horses. Chassie moved in with them just before Carley started night classes in veterinary technology at the community college. Chassie stays home with Dad three nights a week while Carley goes to school. Chassie's still in cosmetology school during the day-time, not dressing any more modestly, but, on the other hand, it's not like Dad can see her. "I like that girl," Dad says, speaking of Chassie, "especially when Mr. Hotpants isn't hanging around. I'm thinking about runnin' him off." The truth may lean more toward how Chassie finds *Bonanza* reruns for Dad, makes popcorn, and tells Dad what's happening on the screen. Unless Frank is there.

Frank looks something like Hoss, and doubtless Chassie prefers the real thing, given a choice. Dad's likely jealous, but when he recites his list of theories about Frank the Predator, naturally Eddie goes berserk.

I've thought Chassie-worry is why Eddie's been acting strange. That, and because we have to go to court with Lana over Rocky. (Both of us would prefer two or three fun-filled root canals.) But last night I was reading in bed when he turned off the television and stuck his face in my hair.

"Something on my mind," he said.

A length of quiet. "What is it?" I prompted. Eddie kept his face in my hair even after he stitched words together.

"Is Carley really okay to give riding lessons? I mean, how she's talkin' about opening the stable in the spring and how Hack's buyin' a colt to train. You really all right with all that? Sounds t' me like no way you're not gonna be all pulled in again . . ." Once it was out, he rolled on his back, sighed, and rubbed his eyes.

"Actually, she wants a filly we can breed later on. It's a start on expanding the herd. She wants to get into training, and Dad and I will teach her. She's chattering about it because she's excited."

"I just don't see it working with her still in school and taking care of Hack, and then you're gonna—"

"Chassie's there to help with Dad. And the stable will only be open weekends. Weekends." Eddie didn't move or uncover his eyes. Frustrated, I went on. "Look, I want this for me, too. I wouldn't mind training a filly of my own, for that matter. Not now, but some-time down the road."

Another sigh from Eddie, blown out long, through puffed out lips.

I worked to strain annoyance from my voice, keep it gentle. "Hey. What's your problem? You've been fine with it, and now you're back worrying. How come?"

"Got used to worryin', I suppose. Afraid to quit. Afraid some-thing'll happen t' make you go nuts with the scissors and me lose you again." He shrugged and shook his head. "Just . . . scared. A lot more'n hair the color of October I love about you, girl. Where's the damn train?"

"What're you talking about?"

Eddie used his elbow to make a tripod. His face was a close-up over me. "Like you don't know. *Who or what would you throw yourself in front of a train for?* Exactly who asked me that?"

Eddie, my Eddie, remembered my standard for evaluating the strength and purity of love? He couldn't have surprised me more if he'd suddenly whinnied while sprouting a mane and tail.

"*You,*" he said. "The answer is you. Yeah, the kids too, but that includes Carley."

I replayed it in my mind afterward as I lay with my legs twined with Eddie's. His mentioning October made me remember my mother's burial, when all the brilliance of the month gathered itself up like a bouquet of scarlet sun. I'm sure Eddie and Carley think the letter from my mother drained the swamp of my anger. Let them believe what they will. It was actually during my mother's burial service that I started to get over being stuck on *nothing is what it seems* and looked at what it might be.

Delia's children were running around like banshees. I have no idea why she let them do that. Perhaps the leaves underfoot releasing their crisp pungency to mix with the moist, dug earth was plain intoxicating to them. Once they got out of control there wasn't much Delia could do short of dashing after them with a lasso and that would have been worse than ignoring them, which is what she did.

In retrospect though, those wild kids did me a huge favor. In gratitude, I should send them enough candy to keep them on a permanent sugar high. Because what they set in motion let me see my own family as I never had.

Naturally, being kids, they couldn't stay away from the grave the cemetery workers had left open mid-job in respect for the service being held. The oldest, Joey, started jumping over it, back and forth. It was distracting, to say the least, because he was right in my line of sight. I closed my eyes to try to concentrate after noticing that Delia and a lot of other people were doing the same thing. It helped that the minister said, "Let us pray."

Suddenly, Joey screamed like he'd seen my mother's ghost. My eyes, and everyone else's, I'm sure, popped open. He was gone. Chloe, his blond-haired little sister, stood three feet away from the hole, terrified. It took everyone seconds to realize that Joey had fallen in. Delia, in purple taffeta and high heels, took off running while the minister valiantly tried to keep going. I was paralyzed next to my mother's coffin. This couldn't be happening. The minister droned on about the Gates of Paradise while Delia charged, squawking and flapping her arms like a panicked goose, and Joey, out of sight, screamed from the grave.

The commotion sounded like it was coming from the Doorway to Hell. I remember covering my eyes, so ashamed that my mother's funeral was turning ridiculous and ruined. At the time I wished I'd thought to stick the barn pistol in my purse. Might as well get good use out of it, and this time I'd make sure nothing blocked my target. I was not in the best place emotionally. Then Eddie, this Eddie who'd done all these things behind my back that I thought were against me, held up his hand and interrupted the minister. "Excuse me. Would you mind waiting a moment?"

The minister stopped mid-sentence on the word *angels*, trailing it out, which my mother would have liked, considering her collection.

Eddie gestured to Cal to follow him. He turned and whispered something to Carley, who grabbed Chassie's hand, and the two girls followed Eddie and Cal. The four of them strode, conferring as they moved in unison to the hysterical scene where Delia was kneeling and carrying on, ineffectually grasping at Joey's scrabbling little hands. Carley hurried to Delia, to get her up and out of the way, keeping an arm around her for support. Meanwhile, the two men stretched out on either side of the hole, reached in, and, on the count of three, lifted Joey up by the armpits, Eddie using only one arm, the other still sore and bruised from my vacuum-wand blow. Chassie was there on Eddie's side to catch the boy and help Carley get mother and son to be quiet, no small feat.

And then Eddie slid back into place by my side, calm as if nothing had happened. His trousers had bits of leaves and brown grass on them, and the side of his jacket probably did too, but he made no show of brushing off. "Please continue," he said to the minister, like a master of ceremonies. The girls were back in place, though Cal stood off to the side, as if he were embarrassed. Delia had the belated good sense to take her children and go home.

They'd all changed sometime during the past months; I was the one who hadn't. Or maybe some different part of them had come forward. A few days after the funeral, Eddie sold the truck that was like his baby. He bought a used Ford Taurus. A week after the funeral, Cal headed for Florida, he said. Eddie denies it, but I'm sure there's a connection between the two. It's best that Cal's left again, but I don't hate him the way I used to. My father says he might not have been any good at cleaning the house, but he cleaned Mama when she soiled herself and didn't make her feel bad about it.

There's more to people than history. There's more than they wear on their faces. Not everyone, most likely, but most.

And now we live on, surprised by unlikely success. I mentioned this to my father recently when I was over there to ride, and he replied, "A blind horse don't *have* to step in every hole, y'know. I sure did at the end with your mother, though. Feel so bad about that. I'm sorry." That's the only time he's made a sideways reference to what she told me in her letter, which he doesn't know about. I hadn't seen a point in reading it to him. I've had enough of recriminations; my own guilt keeps me honest, though accepting it means a sadness and regret that never leaves. When you learn there are mistakes that cannot be fixed and you have made them, well, it does change you.

"And I'm sorry I didn't come see Mama and you," I said, without asking him what he meant. "As you say, *lotsa ways to be blind*. I've got mine, too. So let it go, okay?" It's taken us this long to speak of it even indirectly. If it weighs on him as it does on me, it's heavy.

———

The sweet explosion of grass, the soft air of April. Two pastures alive with scent, movement, birdsong.

The tall, long-legged new Thoroughbred filly, a bright auburn bay, kept her distance until the herd accepted her. Now when she romped, testing the limits, they disciplined her only lightly, even Charyzma. When The Girl, who spent every daylight with them all, first put a blanket on her back, then a saddle, the filly whinnied and Charyzma and Moonbeam nickered to her, *It's all right.* Red and Spice stayed close to the corral with the other two while The Girl crooned and soothed, like Her. The Old Man spent hours with Moonbeam and was often on her back.

Spice heard the noise coming off the road most days now, not like when She didn't come. He carried Her often into the woods where She told him of the wildflowers they passed: violet, bloodroot, trillium, Dutchman's-breeches, blue-eyed Mary, the difference between the five petals of false rue anemone and the six, seven, eight, or nine petals of true rue. One trail ran between the clear wide creek and an uphill slope where a rare patch of true rue was thick as armfuls of tiny fallen stars rising off the earth again. During the time those blooms shone, She guided Spice there daily, where they'd stop a while before her heels signaled him lightly, walk on. On the loop back home, scattered dogwood had their blossoms turned palms up to the sun. Walk on.